Kera Whitt

Otherworld

Kera Whitt

Otherworld

One of nine worlds

JustFiction Edition

Impressum/Imprint (nur für Deutschland/only for Germany)
Bibliografische Information der Deutschen Nationalbibliothek: Die Deutsche Nationalbibliothek verzeichnet diese Publikation in der Deutschen Nationalbibliografie; detaillierte bibliografische Daten sind im Internet über http://dnb.d-nb.de abrufbar.
Alle in diesem Buch genannten Marken und Produktnamen unterliegen warenzeichen-, marken- oder patentrechtlichem Schutz bzw. sind Warenzeichen oder eingetragene Warenzeichen der jeweiligen Inhaber. Die Wiedergabe von Marken, Produktnamen, Gebrauchsnamen, Handelsnamen, Warenbezeichnungen u.s.w. in diesem Werk berechtigt auch ohne besondere Kennzeichnung nicht zu der Annahme, dass solche Namen im Sinne der Warenzeichen- und Markenschutzgesetzgebung als frei zu betrachten wären und daher von jedermann benutzt werden dürften.

Coverbild: www.ingimage.com

Verlag: JustFiction! Edition ist ein Imprint der
LAP LAMBERT Academic Publishing GmbH & Co. KG
Heinrich-Böcking-Str. 6-8, 66121 Saarbrücken, Deutschland
Telefon +49 681 37 20 310, Telefax +49 681 37 20 310-9
Email: info@justfiction-edition.com

Herstellung in Deutschland:
Schaltungsdienst Lange o.H.G., Berlin
Books on Demand GmbH, Norderstedt
Reha GmbH, Saarbrücken
Amazon Distribution GmbH, Leipzig
ISBN: 978-3-8454-4507-6

Imprint (only for USA, GB)
Bibliographic information published by the Deutsche Nationalbibliothek: The Deutsche Nationalbibliothek lists this publication in the Deutsche Nationalbibliografie; detailed bibliographic data are available in the Internet at http://dnb.d-nb.de.
Any brand names and product names mentioned in this book are subject to trademark, brand or patent protection and are trademarks or registered trademarks of their respective holders. The use of brand names, product names, common names, trade names, product descriptions etc. even without a particular marking in this works is in no way to be construed to mean that such names may be regarded as unrestricted in respect of trademark and brand protection legislation and could thus be used by anyone.

Cover image: www.ingimage.com

Publisher: JustFiction! Edition
is an imprint of the publishing house
LAP LAMBERT Academic Publishing GmbH & Co. KG
Heinrich-Böcking-Str. 6-8, 66121 Saarbrücken, Germany
Phone +49 681 37 20 310, Fax +49 681 37 20 310-9
Email: info@justfiction-edition.com

Printed in the U.S.A.
Printed in the U.K. by (see last page)
ISBN: 978-3-8454-4507-6

Table of contents

Set in one of the nine worlds, Otherworld is based on pure fiction. Although, the world Otherworld is a concept in Celtic Mythology. This story contains romance, adventure, and the super natural.

Otherworld

Chapter One: Confusion Is In The Cards For Today

The alarm blaring was what woke me that chilly morning. My aunt Sara usually sets it for me, and she always turns the volume loud enough for me to jump, nearly falling out the bed.

"Gooddd morningg, Yermo, California! It is four o'clock in the morning; 18 degrees outside-" I cut the radio's chipper, loud voice off. Seriously nobody's voice is that happy this early. I groan, unwillingly getting out of my warm, soft bed. Too early to be waking up for school, I grumble in my head, wanting to wrap those inviting covers back around me and snuggle up until I was fast asleep again. I switch on my bathroom light, squinting my eyes at the sudden brightness.

"What the hell?" I gasp at my unusual pale face, unusual because normally it was naturally tanned. A trait I got from my Indian father, or at least that's what Aunt Sara told me. I never knew or will know my parents. The only information I heard of them is what she told me-not very much either-she believed that we shouldn't dwell on the past. That is was unhealthy and unnecessary.

"If we lived in the past, how would we be successful in the present and future? Really, Lakota, you're better off not knowing what happened," she would pull her shoulders back, her head held high. Aunt Sara was always filled with wisdom, strength, and what people called a steel spine. Nothing slowed her down, everyone feared her.

"Strange," I mumble, touching my face lightly, carefully as I were to snap and break into a million pieces. Even my eyes looked strange. I was so used to looking into the mirror and having blue-silver eyes stare back-but these, these are different. Now they were a beautiful purple, shining so brightly and captivating. I don't know who's eyes are these, but heck, I am not complaining. Their far more prettier than my normal ones, I thought, trying to calm myself before I freaked out. Everything is okay; maybe you just thought you had blue eyes and really you never did. No, I argued with myself. I think I would remember my own eye color.

Not bothering to get dress, I rush out my door and down the stairs to find my aunt and ask her opinion about it. "Whoa, slow down, Miss VanHoren," our butler John smiled down at me when I bumped into him. "Are you-feeling okay?" he asked slowly, looking closer at my face.

I sigh heavily, grateful I wasn't the only one who noticed so quickly. "I don't know! I think so. John, are my eyes and face-" I asked, forcing the words out as if I couldn't get them out fast enough.

"Lakota Chloe VanHoren, why are you not dressed already? How dare you come down for breakfast not dressed properly!" she gasped, stopping her feet a few feet away from me. "What did you do?" she whispered, her voice hoarse and dry. Her fingers nervously went to her necklace to twist and untwist it, a sign she was extremely uncomfortable and nervous. I had never, not once in my 17 years have ever seen her so . . .weird. Well, expect for the time her brother died two years ago. Even then, she wasn't as fidgeted as she was now.

"What's wrong with me? I think I'm even a few inches taller. I grew over night," I panicked, playing with my hands. Teenagers pick up bad habits from what they see others doing, I though, trying to focus on anything but me.

John nodded, refusing to meet my eyes, turning to Aunt Sara. "Her cheekbones are higha, she's talla, even her body is ah little curver," his country twang just clear enough for us to ever understand him.

I watched as her face paled even more, she dropped her hand. "John . . ." she left unfinished.

"Right on it, Mrs. VanHoren!" he began walking down the long hallway, leading only to Aunt Sara's office. She cleared her throat, pulling back her shoulders. The surprise was over, she was back.

"Chloe, go finish dressing. When you're done meet me in the sitting room," she turned on her feet, the loud tapping off her high heels vibrating off the walls as she walked back into the dinning room.

I frowned after her, starting back up the stairs. Why had they acted so strangely? Especially Aunt Sara, she looked like she had seen a ghost. Like she had come face to face with something she never wanted to. Not to mention she called me Chloe, my middle name, which I preferred to go by much more than Lakota. It was such an uncommon name, so tribal. Eager to hear what I was into, I rushed into a dark pair of ripped, tight jeans, a plain tee-shirt, a white pullover sweater, and threw on my shoes. After that, I ran back down stairs, following the hallway curves and turns until I reached the cherry wood, double doors that lead to the sitting room. It was my favorite room of all in our old, huge house. Despite the arguments and disagreements, I had to admit my aunt has an eye for fashion. The room was set with matching sitting like couches (I forget the name its actually called) straight from the antique shops in Europe, tan-peach long curtains, and lightly dimmed laps. Before, I couldn't understand why in the freaking world would my aunt keep the lights so low, but more recently, I've become to hate bright lights.

"Okay, what do you want, Aunt Sara?" I asked, walking into the door, annoyed I was running late to school. My English teacher has been on my back from the second I got switched to his class a month ago. He's for sure going to give me a D.T., I thought bitterly.

"Lakota, I'd like you to meet Odin Omay," she smiled, nodding to the guy standing by the bay window. I suppressed a gasp. God, he is perfect! Standing close or at 6 feet tall, his hair was an odd-but beautiful-medium brown with a slight red and blonde tint to it, his pupil's green (not black like normal people!) and the outer a sea foam green. His face looked like as if he were sculpted from a Goddess, the lines were perfectly carved, his skin a smooth, marble texture. His body was muscular but lean, his lips full with a pale pink color. From the casual way he stood, I could tell he was in control and had a certain air of sexuality that proved he could make a woman's knees buckle and collapsed if he so much as barely touched her.

He smiled slowly, eyeing me up and down briefly. "Hello, Chloe. Sara has told me all about you," his sweet but firm voice teased me. "I've read you like to be called Chloe, not Lakota," he added. He read? From where? And why the heck was he so sure of himself and they acted as if he was very important?! Sure, he is beautiful and young, but does that automatically have others give him respect?

"Sarah," he turned to her, clearly accusing her. "You have not told Chloe the truth yet." It wasn't a question, but she answered like it was. "No, I haven't. I wanted her to grow up as if she was normal and belonged in this world. Do you have any idea how hard it is living in the mundane world and knowing you're not apart of them? If I had told her, she would've isolated herself, Odin. It was best for her in this situation," she snapped, surprising me she wasn't affected by him at all. Well, duh, she had iron for blood, I reminded myself. It was a joke I often heard from others, though they never dared to tell her to her face.

He pursed his lips, bringing his long hands out of his pocket. My god, does he even have the slightest clue how far I'm in over? "Yes, well, I'm sure that was what you had thought best for her," he came around to sit on the couch. "I will take over from here. You know what you need to do," he ordered, dismissing her with a flick of his hand. Face red with anger, she stood to her feet. She was not used to being ordered around.

"Very well," she hissed, stopping at the doors. "I will pack Lakota's clothes and personal items," she added with a smirk, closing the cherry wood, double doors behind her.

"What?! She's packing my clothes? Why? Where am I going? I'm not leaving my home," I bit my lip to stop of flooded words I wanted to scream out.

He pointed to the chair in front of him. "Sit, you're making me nervous. You have to leave, Chloe. You don't belong in this world, here roaming around with humans. Your immortal, like me, like your-aunt, your house maids. You should be in Other World, with people of your kind. As for me, I'm different than normal inhumans-I'm part god and vampire. Your aunt is a witchan, a witchan is much stronger than a normal witch by the way. At the moment we are unsure what you are. But we know for a fact your not a human, that's for sure," he smiled again, his unique eyes twinkling.

"Your mother, she was a Goddess Witchan; your father was a vampire. In our world, such an union has never been known and it is illegal to this day. But I think you might be a combination of three. Now, before you can doubt me or claim me insane I'd like you believe me. After all, isn't my face carved like a God, according to you?" he teased me, my face flushing brightly. "I can read minds as well as other talents I'll later tell you of. I will your mentor at Nighting Gale School and your teacher in some classes. I'll teach you how to use a sword, fight like a warrior, educate you on immortal history, and so much more. I have a strong belief you are going to enjoy it there. Why shouldn't you, when it is so breath takingly beautiful? I know this is a rush for you and so confusing, but we have to hurry. I have an important meeting with Zeus that I cannot possibly miss."

I shook my head, trying to clear it. He. Is. Insane. Only a crazy person would think their immortal-

"Chloe, please. We do not have time. I'll explain it you in further detail later," he held out his hand. "Take it," he ordered, raising his voice. Afraid of the sharp tone, I took his hand, unsuccessfully trying to ignore the electric flashes I had throughout my body.

"What are we doing?" I asked, suddenly feeling light headed, my vision bluring. With my free hand, I rubbed my eyes to clear it. Damn. Now my eyes are messing up.

"Your eyes are fine, it's just the magick of switching worlds. You really are going to love Other World," he whispered, clearly excited.

I blinked and suddenly was in another world. A far much more captivating, perfect place. Looking up at the night sky, I became fascinated with the colors for it was very unusual. Blue with a hint of green and purple, three moons barely lit the dark night. One of the moons was red, one bluish white, and another a yellowish green. The stars surrounding them was stunning and dazzling; bright as they could get. The forest below us seemed greener and more alive than the ones back in the human realm, and even more amazing was that at the top of the trees, hiding in the leaves, it was lit by a blue-white light glowing on its own. I blink again and we are standing outside a huge castle. It was tall, standing with five floors and small windows, with pointy, round tops. Some of the rooms had balconies, most didn't.

The building was surrounded by a wall, much like the Great Wall Of China, only not even half as tall. The building of the school was made out of old looking, classic stones from what seemed like the medieval period, maybe older. He opened one of the impressive, tall doors, shutting them softly behind us. Even still, the sound echoed through out the long corridor. The smooth, marble floors were colored in gold, the walls made out of mirrors, the ceiling high enough to fit a giant with chandlers hanging from them. The chandeliers had candles on them instead of light bulbs, like Odin had warned. There was at least two dozen chandeliers lighting the hallway, but it wasn't bright nor was it dark. The ceiling was painted angels and other unknown mystical creatures lined in brilliant colors like gold, white, a strange red, and other odd colors. The hallway was breath taking enough, so I couldn't wait to see the other rooms!

The hallway resembled the Grand Hallway In Versailles, Paris, I thought, walking down the hall until we stopped in front of cherry wood red doors. The doors it self was marvelous, trimmed and cut perfectly designed to match the surroundings. I was more than disappointed to see his ordinary office. It was like any other, only messier. Papers were flung every where from his large desk to his chairs, and even on the floor. "Sorry about the mess. I've been so busy lately, and I'd rather not clean it because like this I know where everything is. It is organized into different topics and whatnot," he explained, cleaning off one of the chair for me. "Sit here while you wait for Is. I'll return shortly," he closed the door behind him.

It was only a few seconds passed when I heard a humph close by me. I turned to see a tall, lean woman with strawberry blonde hair and striking hazel eyes. Though her eyes appeared soft, her face was uninviting and mean looking despite how pretty she was. "I expected more from this little child. I've should've known better," she mumbled, eyeing me up and down, her eyes narrowing for some odd reason. "Stand," she ordered, taking my hand once I did.

I felt odd then, like something or someone was swimming through my veins and deep into my blood. I looked down at my wrist to see them filled with black instead of the normal blue. What the hell is she doing to me?! This is not normal, I shook my head. Then I remembered that nothing in this world was normal, and besides, Odin trusted her so I should too. I relaxed, trying to ignore the odd feeling she was giving me until she suddenly pulling sharply away, hissing at me.

"Be nice Is," Odin warned, placing his hand on her shoulder to calm her. Her eyes were now burning with disgust while her face was turned into hatred and irate. "What did you see?" he asked, in a quiet tone.

She hissed again, pulling her teeth over her lips at me. "Like you don't already know!" she turned to him. "What the hell did you bring to this school? Are you insane, have you lost your mind completely?"

His eyes narrowed, his face still emotionless. "Do not question me," he snarled. "Say out loud what you have discovered so that Chloe will know. She has a right to know what she is."

Without looking at me she stated, "Witch, Goddess, and Vampire. Only it isn't split into halves-she is whole of all three. A disgrace to-"

He held up his hand. "That is all, leave us be. Go onto with what you was doing before you was interrupted." She left, unwillingly, but not before giving me a sharp nasty glare.

"I am sorry for her behavior. Is is still bias to mix breeds and other races, like most of others in Other World," he smiled to reassure me that is was all fine.

"That's great," I grimaced, sitting back down. I was going to be a freak here. The only mixed breed in the all of the history of Other World. My, what fun I'm going to have, I thought bitterly.

"It is up to you whether or not you want to tell people of your heritage. Also, I want you to decide something. There are three different types of daughters (daughters meaning what type of race they belong to. Guys are considered sons of whatever race): Daughter of the moon, which is a vampire, Daughter of the Stars, which is a witch, and Daughter of the Sun which is a werewolf. Out of the two, what do you want to be forever named as?" he asked seriously, stepping a little closer to me.

"What is a mixture called?" I demanded, wanting to claim what I am thoroughly.

He smiled, proud of me already. "There is no name. You are the first, so you are able to call your self whatever you want. Be creative," he encouraged.

It took me only a second to decide. "Daughter of the Lunar Eclipse," I boasted, "sounds good enough for me. He roared with laughter, causing me to frown in confusion. "What is so freaking funny? You don't like my name?" I accused, my feelings hurt. I had thought it was unique and resembled the names of the other races.

"No, no. It's not like that! I lied to you; there IS a name for what you are. You guessed correctly, how odd is that?" he mused, staring at me strangely. "Well, anyways, you are Lakota Chloe VanHoren, Daughter of the Lunar Eclipse. You're classes begin at 5 and end at midnight," he handed my schedule to me.

I glanced quickly over it. "You knew," I simply stated, appalled at him. He shrugged, grinning brightly.

"I had only suspicions," he lied, brushing a feather off his robes. "Drake Malberry is waiting outside to show you around. Oh, and Chloe?" he called.

I turned back to him, watching as he slowly sat at his chair. "Yes?"

"I will have your necklace stating who you are ready for you to wear by the end of the week. As soon as class is out tomorrow, come to my office."

I nodded, closing the door softly. "Hello!" I heard a strong voice hypery say. "My name is Drake Malberry, whats yours?" I looked up to see a tall, young man smiling at me. His hair was a silver-black, his eyes silver with a slight tint to brown to them. His face was round yet lean, his body muscular and well defined even in his lose robes. He's cute, I decided, very cute.

"Lakota, but my middle name is Chloe. You can call me that," I said, hoping he would call me that.

"Okay. You're very beautiful, you must be a vampire or a Goddess," he bluntly stated, making my face turn red. Oh Jesus, he's one of those open people. "Maybe both?" he grinned, looking me over again, only more slowly.

"Okay. You are a pervert," I grimaced, covering my chest. "I am both," I reluctantly added.

He nodded, placing his hands in his pockets. "Thought so. That's my gift-I know things about people before they even say them. Like you, only something's telling me your more than just a Goddess and Witch, I don't know why. I know it's not possible, but really, its aggravating because it keeps screaming it at me."

I sighed. He was going to find out anyways, might as well as tell him. "I'm also a witch. I am a Daughter of the Lunar Eclipse." Surprisingly, this didn't offend him or disgust him.

"Sweet. Welcome to Nighting Gale, the first breed ever of that kind," he teased, offering his arm to me as we walked in the opposite direction in which I came. "What is your last name? Sorry, last names here are more important than first. It's how we know of their family backgrounds without them giving us information."

"That's sneaky," I laughed, taking his arm. "VanHoren is my last name."

He gasped, his eyes wide. "Oo, a VanHoren? It is a pleasure to finally meet one! They are the best assassin's ever to live! Who is your father?" he asked, excitedly.

"I don't know." I bowed my head in shame. God, what an idiot I must be to him not to even know my parents names. "They died after I was born. My aunt, who I used to live with, refused to give me information of them."

He stopped short, then walked again. "I know who you're parents was. Leigh Melrose and Robert VanHoren. That's about all I know of them, but I'd be happy to help you find more about them," he offered, quickly, directing me to a set of stairs. "We could go right now, if you like, to the library. I'm free for the rest of the night, so it wouldn't bother me.

I smiled. He is going to be a friend, I was convinced. Even if he was flirty and blunt, I like him. It was refreshing to meet someone that was open and honest as he is. "If you don't mind . . ." I hesitated, unsure if he really didn't mind.

"Of course not. Anything for you," he smiled, warming my heart. I had a feeling he was dead serious about the last part. "So to the nerdness place we go," he geeky said in a nerdy voice, even adding the sniffling sound, making me laugh.

"How is it here? Like, is it boring or strict?" I was curious now, wanting to know much about my new home. I didn't miss Aunt Sara's authortive tone and watch-full eyes. Very rarely she let me out of the house after 8, even on the weekends. A reason why I constantly snuck out to meet up with my friends in the desert mountains.

"It's okay. Some of the people are much more cruel than the humans, but you'll find sweet ones too. Odin told me how you grew up in the human realm. How was that, to think you was born a human and live with such stupid people?"

Stupid? Humans are not stupid, sure a little slow at times, but who wasn't? "It was okay, I guess. Though I always thought I was different, but never did I think in this kind of way." I chuckled, thinking of it. I had always been faster, smarter, and quicker than the people I knew. I guess being here explained why I had always been so different.

"I couldn't imagine being near mundane's so often. Just thinking of it makes me want to have a quick bite," he licked his lips lustfully. "I hate 'em, but hey, we need 'em to survive so I guess we pretty much got to deal with them. I'm sorry about your parents, by the way," he opened the door for. I liked how the men here held the doors open for women, but it was starting to become annoying.

"Here we are. It looks like any other library, huh?" he asked. He was right, expect this one was much more larger than anyone I've ever seen and the bookshelves looked older and prettier, and held more books. "Follow me," he walked quickly down the aisles, barely glancing at the titles. "No, no, no. Damn, where the hell is it?" he asked, aggravated. "Oh, duh, Drake. It would be in the restricted aisle!" his face brightened. "Sorry, I'm a little slow sometimes."

I nodded, not agreeing or disagreeing. Hearing him speak to his self out loud kind of freaked me out. At home, anyone would be shunned for speaking like that and declared a Witch. "Are we allowed in that area?" The name it self didn't sound like it would be.

"Nah, but who cares? I have the password, thanks to Autumn. You'll like her, she's pretty smart for a witch," he stated, causing me to correct him.

"There's nothing wrong with being a witch. My mother was one and I am one."

He looked back at me, grinning. "You could be whatever you like and I'll be okay with it. But seriously, you'll find that most witches are not very bright. Ah, here we are!" He pulled out a thick old book, blowing the dust off of it. "Book of the Intelligence's," he read, "by Gaver Tomason and Frederick Hollows." He flipped open the book to the first page. "Leigh Melrose."

I was about to ask what was he doing when he sat down the book and it turned magically to the page. "How in the world-"

"Magick. This is her," he picked it back up, briefly looking at it before handing it to me. I took it, my eyes glues to the picture of a very pretty girl. She had silver blonde hair and purple eyes, her face was constructed perfectly, her lips pale pink and full. I had figured my mother would be pretty, but this girl was absolutely stunning! "You look like her, just as beautiful," he whispered," only more so."

I ignored him and read the text out loud. "Leigh Melrose, commonly once known as Silver-Leigh for her hair and personality, graduated from Nighting Gale High with many honors and degrees. She quickly became an Witchan, a leader of a cult called Faverline, a cult that was once famous and the most powerful of them all. Her down fall was falling in love and marrying Robert VanHoren, a vampire from a very well known and respected family. They later moved to Salem where she decided, without approval, that humans should know of witch existence that soon led to the Salem Witch Trials. She declared to the public what she was and other witchs came forward to admit their-selves. Later, she was blamed for the deaths of the witches that died, but before they could arrest her, she and Robert fled to a small town in Virginia.

"Two years after that, the Councile found her and Robert and trialed them both for the deaths of the innocent lives lost in Salem and violating the law of marrying and having relations with another race. They were both hanged shortly after the trial, guilty of both charges, in Cherry Hill." My lips quivered as I fought back the urge to cry. So this was how they were killed. Aunt Sara was ashamed of my parents-because they loved each other and didn't care if it was illegal. It shouldn't be illegal, people should marry who ever they wanted to, my fist tightened drawing blood. Immortals are just as bias as humans are, I concluded and told Drake that.

He looked at me strangely, like I had lost my freaking mind. "Yeahh, I guess so. Huh. I never thought of it that way. Anyways, you want to see your room now? It's really nice compared to the others, even mine. Maybe we should trade," he elbowed me playfully.

"Or we could share," I teased back, laughing at the shocked look he gave me. "I'm kidding, eesh."

"Damn, I was hoping you was serious," he retorted, grinning. "Come on, tease, let's get you to your apartment."

Luckily my 'apartment' was in the same building, according to Drake I was the only student who lived in this building with the teachers. "That's Odin's apartment," he pointed out, it was only a few rooms down from mine. "That's Luke Fascet, the theater teacher's room," it was right across from mine. "I don't know who the rest are," he shrugged, pulling a key out from his pocket.

He handed it to me so I could unlock my new home. Standing close by the doors was my belongings from home and a note laying on top of one of my suit cases. The sitting room was decent size with a small couch and two comfortable looking chairs and a fire place. The walls are red and gold with silver in some places, sliding doors that led to a balcony. "Am I in the right place? Are students suppose to have large rooms like this?" I was confused. Shouldn't dorms be smaller, less elegant? How in the hell could the staff afford to give special treatment like this?!

"Nah, you're lucky. You have a very nice and specially made apartment, like the teachers here. The student rooms have only one bedroom that they share with other roommates. Man, I'd like to know how you got on Odin's good side so I can too. This is nice," he glanced slowly around the room, sighing heavily. "I guess I should let you get settled in. Goodnight, Chloe. Oh," he added, opening the door, "if you get bored you can hang out with me and some friends later. I'll be in building five, on the first level pass the ballroom."

I nodded, not sure if I wanted to or not. "Maybe, I'll see. I have a lot to do," I added, to excuse myself in case I didn't show. He shrugged, closing the door after him. I was happy to finally to be alone. To be able to think and not talk anymore. The way the day had had exhausted me, confused me, and was exciting. 'Chloe,' the letter read in old fashioned cursive handing writing, 'you aunt sent your clothes for you. Some students don't like the fact their clothes remind them of home, so I've enclosed some money for you to go shopping in case you agree with most teenagers ideals. You can go into town whenever you like. Personally, I heard Ontario Mall is what most like, and I'm sure you'll like it too. Sincerely, Odin.'

I shook my head, my eyes widening at the amount he left me. Jesus Christ, he's crazy! Five thousand dollars to go shopping with? There must've been a mistake. Yeah, that's it. He probably meant to write 500 or 50 dollars and accidentally wrote 5,000. I opened my apartments door, walking down to Odin's room. I didn't even have to knock on it before he opened it, shock written on his face. "Oh, sorry to bother you. Are you on your way to some where?" I asked, not wanting to impose.

"No, no. Oh," he pulled his head back as if I had said something else. "No, Chloe, there was no mistake. Please, take the money. It is nothing to me, I have so much and have no clue how to spend it or what on. Your aunt refused to give you money, so I did. End of discussion," he smiled, making my heart beat out of control. He is perfect, so beautiful! The best part was he didn't seem to realize it or care. Most guys would take advantage of his looks and be arrogant about it.

"Thank you, Mr. Omay," I shyly said, grateful for what he did. His lips twitched to the side, teasing me even more.

"You can call me Odin, Chloe. Here, we either call teachers by their first name or last, no Mr. or Mrs."

I smiled, offering my hand as if it was the first time we meet. "Nice to meet you, Odin. I'm Chloe."

He laughed, taking my hand and shaking it, then folding his arms back. "Nice to meet you too."

Looking at his face I couldn't help but wonder how old he is. He owned the school, so he had to be at least 25, but he didn't look that old. There's no way he's any older than 20, I thought, hopefully. "How old are you?" I blurted, then bit my lip.

"I'm not supposed to say, but I will say I'm more than just seven centuries old," he added, unsure for some reason. There's no way! He looks too young! "Chloe, if I did show my age, how would someone be able to look that old?" he laughed, "I changed into a vampire at 22, so I'm forever stuck at this age."

I smiled happily, though I felt bad he would never grow old, never die. Life was awesome, sure, but who wanted to live forever and ever? "Exactly," he nodded, agreeing with my thoughts. Great. His mind reading was going to be annoying.

"You know, the whole having-no-privacy-and-having-my-mentor-read-my-mind is not agreeable," I grimace at him. He ran his fingers threw his hair, smoothing it back.

"Yeah, if I could help it I would. Sorry," he said apologizing, folding his arms back across his chest. "Or maybe I can and I just don't want to."

My teeth gritted together while my fist tightened. "You better be able to help it!" I yelled at him, storming back to my room, slamming the door. "Men," I hissed. I threw his letter in the trash can. This is going to be a long year.

"Hey, what's so wrong with men?" I heard someone ask. Sitting on my couch was Drake. "What the hell are doing here?" I snapped. He shouldn't be in my apartment without my permission. He held his hand up in defense. "Sorry, the door was unlocked and I didn't want to stand in the hall way to watch you flirting with Odin anymore, so I let myself in to wait for you." His eyes were wide, as if I had done the worst thing ever.

"I wasn't flirting with him," I grumbled, sitting next to him on the couch. He rolled his eyes, leaning back.

"You sure are convincing. Bullshit, you was leaning into him and smiling like a love sick puppy. Whats worse is he was flirting back." He made gagging sounds. I smacked him on the back of his head playfully, but kind of serious.

"You're imagining things! He is my mentor and that's all." He rolled his eyes, taking my hand. His hand was cold while he lightly traced my hands.

"I don't know why but I sorta feel connected to you," he mumbled under his breath, his eyes focusing on our hands. "From the second I saw you, I knew you was special. Am I imagining that?" his eyes met mine intensely. I felt like his eyes were trying to read into my mind or at least my soul. It was unnerving, but at the same time comforting.

"Probably. Was you dropped on the head as a baby?" I tried to hold a straight face, until he busted out laughing. His laugh was soft and sweet, like him. "Why'd you come back?" He let go of my hands to play with his zipper on his coat. "I don't know. I didn't want to leave you alone. Besides, my friends were getting on my nerves. They kept asking so many questions about you and making rude comments to me."

"Like what?" Crap. They probably said I was ugly or stupid, or maybe they thought I was disgusting since I'm a mixed breed. That made me mad. How could they judge me so quickly when they didn't know a thing about me? I haven't said one word to any of them or seen them! It was unfair.

"Nothing bad, really. They saw you when we was walking out of the library. They think your beautiful, its just . . . well, they teased me about you. They said they'd love to hit it and quit it, and other rude, perverted things. I didn't like them talking about you like that so I told them off and came up here," he shrugged. He defended me? Hell, he barely knew me and yet he yelled at his friends, friends I'm sure he knew for a while.

I was glad he stood for me but upset he probably made his friends mad. "You should not of done that. They will be mad at you." He snorted, like it was impossible for that to happen.

"You'll find out that at this school, no one ever stays mad at me or tells me off. They are too scared to do that." He grinned evilly. Something told me I didn't want to know why so I ignored the remark and changed the subject, yawning.

"What time is it?" I suddenly wanted to crawl into bed and sleep for a week, I was so tired. I struggled to keep my eyes open. Stay awake, I told myself. Wait until he leaves to go to sleep. Damn, I was glad he was here, but I want to snuggle up under my covers.

"1 o'clock. I'll let you be. Goodnight, Chloe. Sweet dreams," he whispered, leaning down to kiss my forehead. "I'll be here tomorrow to escort you to your classes, even though the witches will be throwing daggers at me for being in their building," he laughed, clearly over joyed by this.

I nodded, standing to my feet. "Night, Drake. See you," I mumbled, opening the door to

my bedroom and collapsing on my bed, not bothering to change into my nightgown.
Chapter Two: The Sky Is Low and The Clouds Are Mean
I slept soundlessly, my body falling asleep the second I hit the pillow. It was nice, to
finally sleep without nightmares or dreams, to just sleep. A loud knocking woke me,
pounding hard, rapid banging. "Hold on," I mumbled, grinding the sleep out of my eyes.
The curtains covering the windows did not tell me if I had slept through the day or it was
morning.
"Jesus, I've been knocking on the door forever," Drake complained. He was casually dress
in dark blue jeans and a tight-but sorta loose-white, plain shirt. Even still, the ordinary
outfit looked great on him. His lips twitched into a teasing mockery. "I mean, yeah, it's
great to dream about me and not want to wake up, but damn, your impossible to wake."
I rolled my eyes. "You wish. I didn't dream about anything last night so ha."
His eyes twinkled, a sparkling silver-gray. He looks even cuter when he's up to
something, I noted. "Everybody dreams. Sometimes we don't remember them, but we
always dream. It's a proven fact," he boasted proudly.
"Aren't you the nerd," I narrow my eyes at him. From the hints he gave me, I would of
never guessed he was. He sounded like the bad guy type, not the
Italkshitbutreallyl'manerddeepdowninside syndrome.
"Nah, I heard it off of some T.V. show," he shrugged. "Uh, you better get dresses. Your
classes start in a hour, and I still have to show you around so you don't look like a total
dweeb, lost and confused."
I grimaced. Seems no matter where you go, you'll always have high school. I was a bit
thrown off on the T.V. thing but I let it drop. It must be some kind of program here.
"Fine." I carried my suitcases into my room, unzipping the first one, picking out blue
jeans and a sweater.
"You have to wear school uniform," he called from the living room. "Check in your
closet-there should be some there."
The uniforms were . . . Okay, to put it nicely. The robes were long, jet black, and loose
enough to fit all and made not to hint at what genitals were underneath. Could be worse, I
guess. On the front above the breast pocket was written Daughter of the Stars and had
pretty little stars drawn below it. The stars itself looked to have an inner light and was
shining as if it was real. To the touch it felt what a star might feel like; warm, bumpy but
smooth, and shined when ever I ran my fingers across it.
Once I was dressed in it, it didn't look not even half as bad as I thought it would. The blue
tint made my black hair stand out even more. I was a little proud of my features. My
thick, long hair was so dark it appeared to have a little purple in it, my purple-pink eyes
compliments my hair even more, my cheek bones high and defined, my skin lightly
tanned all year long with a slight reddish tint I had received from my Indian side.
"Do I look okay?" I asked him, stepping out of my room. He whistled, giving me a twice
look over, smiling largely.
"Hell, you look more then okay. You're beautiful, not mentioned those morbid robes look
amazing on you more than any other witch I've ever seen." His compliments made the
blood rush to my face. I have never taken words easily and most likely never will. He
seemed to throw around compliments so easily as if it were a normal thing here. Vanity is

a sin. I wonder if they believe in the same religious thoughts here?

"Quit it, Drake," I shyly replied, crossing my arms over my chest. The look in his intense eyes only made me blush worse. He took a step forward, then stopped, unsure of himself. "I'm serious. You are the true definition of exquisite. Give me my heart back," he growled. His words my heart pitty-patty against my chest fastly. I was almost sure he heard it from the way he smugly smiled.

"You have your schedule?" he asked once I locked the door behind us and started down the stairs.

"Yeah," I pulled it from my pocket, unfolding it and giving it to him.

"First period Spells and Charms with Madame Halls. Second is Etiquette with Faser. Third is Rituals with Dahmer. Fourth is Marital Arts, Yamone. Fifth is History, VanRose. Sixth is Social and Debates, Odin. Seventh is Physical Training," he said in a teacher-like voice. "Sweet, you have three classes with me."

I shook my head, confused. Shouldn't I have Algebra and English and other classes like that? These sounded like a walk in the park, an entertainment, not normal classes. "Easy-peasy classes," I smugly said, confident I was going to ace them easy enough.

"Sorry, kid, there a lot harder than you think. Watch and learn. Oh, and we have Social with werewolves," he sneered in disgust, like we were to be surrounded by leprosy. That ticked me off. He was okay with being friends with a hybrid, but not werewolves? What the hell? I silently wished that all the others wasn't so hypocritically racist.

The rest of the hour went by quickly. Drake was very useful, showing me where all my classes would be at, even the bathrooms, theater room, gym room, work out place, library in the buildings, computer room, and so on. Some people stared curiously at me, 'who is this new girl Drake is walking with?' their faces seemed to ask. A few witches smiled at me and carried on with their business-but the vampires glared hatefully once they saw my robes. A vampire was hanging with a witch, an now obvious thing not to do.

We retracted to my first class, standing outside the door. I had two minutes before it started.

"Have a nice day, Chloe," he took my hand, whispering, pulling me a little closer to him so we was only a few inches apart. "Don't take any crap if people tease you for being the new kid."

I smiled lightly. He hadn't need to worry about that! I've always been quick to defend myself, blunt to the extreme, sometimes even being a little too cruel. "I won't, Drake. When will I see you again?" I asked, not wanting to leave him so quickly. I was hoping we would hang out a few hours before school started.

"I have fifth class and so on, with you. I'll see you then." He hesitated, not wanting to leave either. "Are you sure you'll be fine?" his worry consuming his face. That pleased me, that he would be so caring when he barely knew me. "I know, it seems kinda weird and all-but I don't want to have to stress out, wondering if you're fine. I feel like I've know you for years, not a day," his eyes were intense again. I shifted uncomfortably, his eyes wandering me made me feel like he was trying to undress me with his eyes. "I really want to get to know you a lot better," he stressed the word a lot.

Odin told me that this would be illegal, to date or marry other species. "We-I can't. Isn't it illegal for me to?" my voice showed my confusion.

"No, you're a vampire too. Here, because our blood is stronger or whatever, you can't be half Goddess, half witch, half vampire, Chloe. You are full blooded all of those things, that's why you're so special and unique. It was impossible for that to happen and survive it, but you proved scientist wrong. You lived to normal, healthy, and unfairly beautiful," his hand brushed my hair back, lingering in it for a second before pulling away, sighing heavily. "We are allowed to date, even marry if we wanted to. Not many would approve, but that doesn't make it illegal."

I nodded, not knowing what to say. I hoped to God he didn't have any intention about the marriage part. He's sexy, witty, down-to-earth, and calm, but I wasn't sure if I wanted to date him just yet. In the future I could see us dating, sneaking out and making out, and getting close. Just then, I wanted that closeness with him very much. I had never been close with a guy before-I was too shy to-but being around Drake made me want to give it a shot.

The bell ringing pulled me out of my thoughts. He's staring at me with that lustful look again, I nervously thought. His arms wrapped around my waist, pulling me closely to him, giving me a quick kiss on the forehead. "Good day, Chloe. I'll see you soon."

Chapter Two: The Sky Is Low and the Clouds Are Mean

"Oh, hello, Miss . . .?" Madame Hall asked. She was average looking with blonde hair and soft, almond-shaped green eyes. She was short and tiny, like a young teenager.

"Lakota VanHoren," I shook her hand. She smiled brightly, her smile resembling a diamond glittering in the sun.

"Ahh, you must be the Daughter of the Lunar Eclipse," she announced, causing other students to suddenly look at me with curious looks. I was positive they never heard of such a thing. Only Daughter's of the Sun, Stars, and Moon were ever created.

"Yes," I uneasily stated, though it wasn't really a question. She nodded, indicating I should sit in the only open seat. In this class, we had round tables and the room was cloaked in darker but pretty color's of black, purple, dark blue, a splash of red and yellow and green. The room itself was dimmed lightly, giving only enough light to see, and smelled of a sweet, refreshing smoke.

"It's called sage, my dear. I like to purify and cleanse my rooms of evil things," she stared out around the room, her eyes lingering and narrowing on some of the students. I saw them shift nervously, quickly looking away with guilt painted over their faces. "Please, sit by Autumn Darkwood in the back. Poor thing, she usually sits by herself since we didn't have any extra students," she gave the blonde in the back a sympathy look before returning to her desk.

"Hiya, I'm Autumn," she peppily stated, nearly hoping down in her seat. "Where are you from? Whats your name? What class do you have next? Oo, I hope you have Sanders! I have that class, wait. Not until third," she giggled, covering her mouth with her hand very ladylike.

Autumn was pretty. She was short and tiny, with striking blonde-chestnut hair down to her shoulders, waving perfectly in all the right places, bright sky blue eyes on a summer day, smooth peaches and cream complexion. Her hands were child-like, her body reminding me of a Barbie doll under a magnify glass. Her overly hyper attitude matched her perfect looks accordingly.

I laughed, overwhelmed by all her questions. "I'm Lakota VanHoren, but I like to be called Chloe. I'm from California. What was the rest of the questions?" She had fired so many at me, I couldn't keep up.

Her eyes widen in surprise and joy. "The human world? Oh my goodness, you are so freakin' lucky! Seriously, your the only one here that is from there. What was it like? Did you know you was different from the humans? I never got to visit yet; you have to be with an Elder to go there if your under 17," she grimaced, then her face brightened again.

"Have you gone into town yet? The malls there are boring, but there's this one-I forget the name, whatever-I adore it! The clothes are truly awesome."

I shook my head, trying miserably to stop from laughing. "You are extremely hyper. Do you have A.D.D.?"

She pretended to think for a second, cocking her head to the side before grinning at me again. "Hmm, you know what? I think a few, overpaid doctors have claimed that but shoot, I'm not hyper," she innocently replied. "I'm very calm and collected," she placed her hands on the table folding them together, her spine straighten like a good little student.

"Okay, miss drama queen," I giggled. I'm going to like this one, I thought, sure of it. Her emotions flipped a lot like she was turning on and off like a light switch, adjusting to her whenever she felt to change them. But overall, she was nice and charming without being preppy or annoying.

"Class, settle down. We have much to do today. Well," the teacher pursued her lips in thought, "I guess it's the same as any other day. Anyhow, turn your book to page 97. We'll be learning how to break spells that someone put on you. The Gritzle," she explained, pulling out materials from her desk.

"Here," Autmun offered to share her book with me. 'The Gritzle is commonly used to ward of simple, easier spells. Mix dry thristle wood, lavendar, fox sage, hoover candle wax, and a drop of blood into a wooden bowl,' the direction read. A drop of blood? Are they friggin' insane?! Who's blood, mine or something the teacher was going to hand out?

"Now class, do not frit-you will have to poke yourself with a pin to get the blood. It is what's used for spell breaking, and if you want to become a powerful, strong witch you have to follow the directions to heart," she wagged her finger. "You may begin, using the materials on your desk."

"Do you want to draw your blood or should I?" she asked, already starting on mixing the ingredients into the round bowl.

"I will," I muttered, not really wanting to do it. "Ouch," I jumped, removing the pin from my skin. "What the hell?" I looked down at my finger to see a thick, silver thing coming out where the blood should be. It immediately filled my nose; the smell of sweet, tangy, mystical smell. It luring me into it, wanting to suddenly taste the silver strange thing. Autumn gasped, wakening me from the daze.

"Madame," she shakingly said. She followed to our table. "Look. What is it? It smells so-beautiful. I ain't no vampire, but I would kill to taste it," her voice even seemed dazed, her eyes dilated.

"Oh, no need to worry. You're a Goddess, correct? Their blood is of that colour and smell," Madame smile reassuring me, lightly tapping my hand. "Congratulations. You are truly an Immortal."

I heard snickering and whispers around me. "She's a Goddess? The bitch! It's not fair," a unknown girl hissed behind me. Another said," I heard she's also Vampire, too. Freaky, right? Is-Is told Josh and he told me. What a fucking freak," someone laughed.

"Thank you, Madame. So it seems some are jealous enough that they already talking about me in a two-faced way. What a shame; my friend was right how witch's are quick to judge," I innocently retorted so that everyone heard me. Good. That shut them up.

"Yes, well, keep working," Madame smiled before returning to her desk.

"Nice one," Autumn grinned, like a proud mother just hearing her child is on honor roll. "Give 'em what they deserve. I know I did, when I was new here, that's why they don't like me," she shrugged, indifferent to what they thought. "Do I care? Nope, not one ounce-and it drives them crazy."

My classes went by fast-it seemed not shortly after I sat in my chair, the bell was ringing again. Autumn was helpful and her usual, hyper self, ignoring the dirty glances the students was giving us. Like Autumn, I didn't care too much about what people thought about me. People will think of what they will want, no matter how much you try to convince them, so what's the point in even trying to? Just as I was walking to fourth period, my vision became blurry, my knees weak.

"Autumn," I cried, my hands out trying to blindly reach her. By now I couldn't see a thing, total blackness. I didn't like this. At all. "Sit me down someone. Quick," I snapped, her hand grasping mine and pulling me forward -I think- and sitting me on a bench.

"Chloe, whats-" her voice slowly faded out until I could no longer hear it. Instead was replaced with loud, cheerful laughter as I saw me, Autumn, Drake, an unknown average, brown hair boy, and a pretty black haired girl. I sensed that it was like a group, a common thing for them to hang out daily. I didn't know why but I had the strange feeling we shouldn't be so close, yet we were and treated as outsiders, even Drake who was the popular guy. But we didn't care, at all, we was happy in our closed friend group.

The scene changed to a different one-less vibrant. I was fighting in a war, I think, against another unknown man. We were fighting with swords, ready to kill the other. All around us death loomed in the air as massive people were fighting for their own lives. Drake turned to me, mouthing I love you. His loving eyes turned to shock, sadness, and then hatred as he raced towards the man I had been fighting, quickly killing his enemy in one swift movement.

I looked down to see blood gushing out of my stomach, it was that pretty silver color. "Drake," I gasped, falling to the ground, removing the blade out of me. Funny, it didn't hurt as much as I thought it would. Seeing Drake's face hurt more than anything else.

"Help," I chocked out, the tears falling down my face.

His arms wrapped around me tightly. "I'm not going to let you die. I'll change you."

The scene fades again, until I was back in present time. Autumn's pale face freaked me out, she stood looking at me in shock. "What, what's wrong?" I shakily asked, still feeling weak from whatever I had just saw. Maybe I was dreaming while I was awake. Or something like that.

"Nothing. You should go see Odin-you're going to need his help. Now," she pulled me to my feet, taking my arm into hers. I breath sharply, trying to regulate it back to normal, to calm my shaking knees.

"I'll be fine," I snapped. Unsuccessfully, I tried to get away, only to make myself weaker and more drained. "Okay, let's go see him," I gave in. I wanted this feeling to go away. I like being in control of myself, to be able to clear my thoughts and not rely on others. I felt so useless, so ashamed. "I'll go," I change my mind, wanting to be strong. With a yank from her arms, I pull away, taking a step forward then everything went black.

"Ughh," I groaned, my hand pressing to my forehead. "My forehead hurts like hell."

"It's about time you're awake; you're savior was starting to worry," Odin laughed. I open my eyes to see the God leaning over me. Very casually he removed my hand to replace it with a cold, wet towel. "The pain should start to dull here soon. Your lucky Drake was there to save you when you collapsed outside of your last class. Autumn told me what happened and all, but I'd like to hear from you what happened. I have a pretty good idea what is was," he added, sitting back onto his chair next to my bedside. I was in a hospital room, or at least what resembled one. A hideous white, paper gown glued to my skin and smelled like plastic.

"I don't really know. One minute I was talking to Autumn, the next I was day dreaming of people I've never met before, the scenes flashed quickly but not enough so I didn't know what was happening." The happy scenes replayed in my head, the joyful times with the people. The other one, the not so happy one, forced its way back into my head, reminding me of the-no it wasn't possible. It was just a day dream. That's all it was.

"It wasn't a dream, Chloe. You had visions, visions of what may happen in the future, depending on what you choose," he reached out for my hand, then pulled away before it touched mine. "You can see the future, a very rare gift. In fact, I think the last to be able to see was your father, a hundred years ago," he smiled faintly.

"So-my death, it's possible I'd be killed in a war?" my voice raised a few notes higher than I wanted to. "I'm going to serve in a freakin' war? And be killed?! Where the hell are you to save me? Aren't you suppose to change me or something like that? You wasn't there in the 'vision' only Drake was! Some mentor you are," I hissed, angry. I didn't want to die, not now. Not when I had so much to look forward to. The tears in my eyes filled them, threatening to spill over any second.

His head bowed, hiding his face from me. "I will not let you die. As for this war, what do you think will cause it?"

Of all things to talk about right now, and he choose this. "I don't know!" My forehead screamed back at me, telling me to keep my voice down or pain was going to spread again.

"Yes, you do. Don't think about it, just say whatever comes to," his eyes met mine. He's so beautiful, so damned striking! It wasn't fair he was so far beyond my reach, only there to tease me but to never touch.

"Me," I blurted, then gasped. It was true. I know I'm going to be the one who starts it. But why? Why would I go to war with anyone?

He took the i.v. out of my hand, careful not to spill any blood. I don't blame him; the blood itself is too powering and strong. "That's what I'd like to know. You must have a good reason to, in the future I'm sure. Time will tell," he sighed, looking down over me. My headache was coming back, a stabbing pain in my temples. I swear I could feel my

heart beat pounding from my head as the blood rushing in it and caused more ache.
Wait. He said a hundred years ago. My dad probably wasn't even born then. "A 100 years ago?"
He looked away. "Yeah, you were born that long ago. You didn't start growing until 17 years ago. You lived with me. I took care of you until then, your great-great grand niece took over later," he shrugged, a serious face painted on him. He wasn't lying. I knew he wasn't.
"I'm not a 100," I stubbornly denied. There was no way I could be, even if he was telling the truth. Hell, I didn't look no where near it!
His eyes rolled to the ceiling then back on me. He laughed before saying, "Chloe, do I look my age? No. And neither do you. Now quit arguing and accept the truth. Ask Drake to look it up for you in the library. You need your rest," he got to his feet unwillingly.
After that, the rest of the week went by fast. I didn't have another vision, and I was already used to my classes. Drake was overly concerned when I finally left the school's hospital and returned to my apartment.
"I thought I had lost you," he murmured, his eye's turned to the window, boringly staring out at the pretty scenery. "Well, until I felt you're pulse." I had laughed, telling him how silly he was.
I was accelerating at a fast speed in all my classes; I had already passed my fellow students, which shocked all my teachers. One day after history with Luke VanRose, he asked me to stay after class.
What have I done now? I groaned in my head. Damn. I knew I should've stuck to the homework's directions and not do it my way. I'm such a nerd and a screw up. My first week here and I've already made enemies, passed out, and now this!
"You're not in trouble," his tone revealed his amusement. He closed his book, standing to his feet to walk over to me. VanRose is tall-like most vampires are, I have noticed-with jet black hair and green eyes. I have heard enough whispers and gossiping to know that most of the girls here have a crush on him. The way he grinned, flashing a cute dimple on his left cheek, I understood why they like him so much. He is sexyy and something about him screamed bad-ass.
"Then why-" I began, confused, but his words cut me off.
"I read over you're homework you turned in today. It was simply stunning! How do you know so much of the history of the human realm?" He took a step forward, our bodies are only a foot away from the other.
"I lived in the human realm, up until a week ago, VanRose," I politely replied, trying to ignore the sleek, lustful look in his eyes. His eyes slowly trailed down my body, then up, then back down again. I blushed, turning my head away so he wouldn't see.
This is not happening, I tried to convinced myself. You're teacher is not hitting on you.
"Ahh, yes. So I have heard, but I don't believe the gossip this school says. They also say you and Drake are already 'hitting it off,' so to speak." Was that jealously I heard? "Is that true?" he demanded, raising my chin to look up at him.
His eyes are soft and full of an emotion I couldn't comprehend. "We are friends, that is all. But he has admitted to liking me," I blurted, wanting to tell him anything he asked of me, then bit my lip.

Seriousness took over his face, dropping his hand to his side. "Do you like him?"
I frowned, not seeing where this was going. "What business is it yours?" I sneered, not
liking the tone he had. He is my teacher, not a friend I could talk about stuff like this to.
He took my hand, sending butterflies throughout my stomach. I ignored them, trying to
pull my hand out of his. "I don't want you with him. He is not good, something about him
tells me he is not truthful, Lakota, I mean Chloe," he corrected quickly. "Stay away from
him."
The hell I would! "No. Drake has nothing to hide, he has not been lying to me. He has
been there enough for me already to know this. He-"
"Yes, yes," his hand waved the subject away. "I know this, too. I'm warning to stay away
from him, Chloe. I don't-you should be careful around him," he warned, lightly brushing
my cheek. I stared up at those deep, sparkling green eyes, unable to pull them away as his
hand rested on my cheek.
"What's it matter to you anyway?" I softly whispered, as if someone might over hear, even
though we were the only ones left in this entire building. The silent atmosphere confirmed
this, not a heart beat radiated through the halls. I unwaringly leaned in closer to him, my
own heart thumping loudly, almost too fast for my body to catch up with it.
"I wouldn't want to see you hurt. Plus, not to mention the amount of hell I'd get from Odin
if someone was to be put in a coma state from me," he chuckled, referring to hurting
Drake. He likes me, a wave of tremor shot throughout my body. He's not suppose to, I
reminded myself. Oh, to hell with the rules, I snapped back, wanting to suddenly throw
myself in his arms.
"Erh, thank you, but I wouldn't need help," I stammered idiotically. Great. I make myself
look stupid again. "I have to go," I cried when his face inched closer to mine, scooping up
my shoulder back pack. "See you Monday!" I called out, acting like I didn't hear him
calling out after me.
I ran in to something hard, causing me cuss and fall backwards onto my buttocks. "What
the hell?" I hissed, gathering quickly back to feet.
"I'm so sorry, miss! I was running, I have to go to D.T. and I didn't know anyone was left
in this building," a young man explained, his face written with regret. He instantly
reminded me of a bear, but cute and overly adorable. His hair brown, a chocolate color,
eyes an odd white and blue. He is the most muscular guy I have ever met without over
doing it. I jumped, he's the guy from my vision! The one I saw with me and Drake and
Autumn! Only he smelled . . .different from me and everyone else. His skin was a strong
forest and autumn air smell, but it was very pleasant and refreshing.
"It is fine, don't worry about it. I saw you, you're from my vision I had a few days ago," I
blurted, not wanting to waste any time. Instead of looking at me crazily or walking away,
he smiled lightly.
"Oh, and what was this vision I was in?" he casually asked, placing his hands on his back
pockets.
"It was me, you, Drake, Autumn, and some other girl all hanging out. I could sense we
were all close friends, a small group," I shrugged, grinning.
He laughed, his shoulder bobbing up and down. "That is not possible," his eyes turned
sad, all light leaving them.

"Why not?" Did he think he was too good for us? Sure, that was it. His size proved he is a jock, and I was willing to guess even here jocks didn't hang with my kind. I was pissed as my mind registered this. "You think you're too good for me?"

His head snapped up, confusion planted on his face. "You cannot be serious. Me? No, I'm just a mangy dog. If anything, your too good for me to be around. Plus, you're Drake wouldn't like to be near werewolves," his smile was false. He. Is. Not. My. Drake. What the hell was he telling everyone? Note to self: kill Drake later.

"Screw what Drake has to say, and he is not my Drake. He is my friend and only that! Now, Odin said vision, so it will come true. You have no say in it so you might as well as accept it willingly or else," I threatened playfully. He laughed, his shoulders shaking again.

"You have a temper, eh?" he chuckled, his shoulders sagging in defeat. "Fine, you win. I warn you, people will not like you talking to me. Vampires and werewolves do not blend."

I clapped my hands dorkishly. "Excellent. Meet me after your D.T. here. Like I said before, the heck with what others have to say. I will do as I please, and I don't care if your a werewolf or a demon. You are going to be my friend, so get used to it." I grinned, shaking his hand.

He shook his head. "This was a strange meeting miss . . .?" he asked, trying to hide his amusement.

"Chloe VanHoren. You?"

His jaw dropped for a second, then he gulped nervously. "Dylan Woodruff, don't laugh!" I couldn't help it-his surname fitted perfectly. "Ruff, ruff?" I giggled, we both busted out laughing, our sounds echoing down the halls.

"Woodruff!" someone yelled, irate. It was an unknown teacher, with her hands on her hips. "You are late and I find you mingling with another student? You are disobedient and incorrigible, as usual. Now, get in my class!" she yelled, causing Luke to come out of his class.

"What is going on?" he addressed me, barely glancing at the other teacher.

"Mind your own business, VanRose. Woodruff," she called, nearly snapping, turning back to her room.

He grimaced after her, then turned to me. "The warden calls. See you later, Chloe." I nodded, shaking my head at Luke. "Some teacher's are too unfair," I barely was audible, but I knew he heard me.

"Hey," someone called from behind me. I turned fast on my heels, hoping it was Drake. It wasn't, much to my disappointment. I faked a smile when Dylan's face dropped at my reaction.

"The warden finally released you?" I asked, though my mind was else where. Damn, where is that woman? She's always late for everything. If she isn't here in two more minutes, I warned, my thoughts being cut off.

"Sup, Chlo'," a cheerful, bright voice came from the tiny, little devil suddenly two feet away from me. She had changed from her uniform into something so bizarre, so-werid, but pretty, like her. A cut short skirt hung from her hips, strange black tights underneath the skirt, with a bright pink shirt that read 'Peace, Love, Unity, and Respect' in bold, black letters. Her hair was swept back in a loose pony tail with a few pieces hanging out by her temples, showing off unmatching earrings. One was purple, squared, and flat against her ear, the other was round and large with black squares and rainbow colored strips. Her shoes were flats and lime green and a shiny purple. If someone else to wear this outfit, people would look at them like they were crazy or something.

But not Autumn. It . . .looked right on her. Only she could pull this flashy, eye snatching, bold look and do it so well. "Nice outfit," I grinned. "It looks great."

She glanced down as if she didn't remember what she was wearing then shrugged. "Yupp. Is-Is assured me it would be the style in a hundred years or so. Anyhoo, I came up with the lovely idea first and I simply adored the brightness. Oh, who are you? Chloe, what are we doing today?" she asked innocently, hoping off subject as she normally did so quickly. I smiled to myself, enjoying the bright, hyper Autumn I've come to be very close to.

"I'm Dylan," he blushed, eyeing her up and down then looked away guiltily. She offered her hand to shake but he stared at it until she coughed nervously and dropped it.

"I don't know," I answered her question from earlier. "Where do you want to go?"

'She's pretty; too bad she's a witch.'

"Hmm, did you say something Dylan?" I asked, barely noticing what he had said.

"I didn't say anything." I turned my eyes to him, his face was serious. Autumn was looking at me strangely.

"Oh, I must be hearing things," I muttered, knowing dang well he had said that. Fine, he want's to play dumb, let him. I know he likes Autumn, I heard him. Right? I mean, it was a litter lower than what he his normal voice was, and much softer, but it was him nevertheless. He had said it, I stubbornly hung on to, not wanting to let it drop inside my head. He's just embarrassed to admit it in front of her, that's all.

"What do you think?" Autumn asked, snapping me out of my thoughts. I missed a conversation from being so warped in my head.

"I wasn't listening, what was you saying?" 'God, she can be such a blonde sometimes,' I heard Autumn say lowly. "I'm not a blonde!" I defended, only a little offended.

Her eyes grew wide, scared almost. "I didn't say that out loud," she hoarsely replied, looking concern for me. "Chlo', I only said that in my head."

I looked at Drake then back to her. Surely I had missed something. She did say it. Or didn't she? I wasn't so sure anymore. "I'm confused.."

Dylan cleared his throat. "Can you read minds?" he bluntly asked, shocking me with it.

"No, or at least I don't think so," I wrinkled my brows together. Read minds? Noo, I couldn't. I already had a gift. Hybrids couldn't have another, could they?

"What did I just say that made you think I said you are a blonde?" Autumn whispered, seeming to already know.

"You said that I can be a blonde sometimes. Right? Isn't that what she said?" I turned to Dylan, needing reassurance.

He shook his head, smiling. "Nope, I didn't hear it. Congratulations, you can read minds!" he appalled for me. "You must be-"

"Try to think of what I'm thinking," Autumn ordered. I closed my eyes in deep thought. 'I miss the after smell of rain and the Opry.' I opened my eyes and told her that.

She clapped her hands together, smiling. "Excellent. Then it's settled; you can read minds.

No if and buts," she added when I opened my mouth. "Now, what should we do today? Look the sun is setting!" she pointed to the most stunning sunset I've ever saw. The clouds were outlined with green, gold, and blue. The sky itself was an amazing shades of bright red, orange and pink. Now I could understand how people said sunrise's and sunset's make them feel happy . . .Looking at this one I couldn't help but to be filled with love and happiness and a wonderful feeling that made me feel more alive than ever. It was that pretty.

"The vampire's will be coming out soon," Dylan muttered under his breath. "Strange, the human concept tells them that vampires cannot come out during the day, which is true for some in their world-something about there sun is stronger or whatever-but here, the sun cannot hurt them. Yet, they stay inside until it is dark. Chloe, why is that?"

I shrugged, tearing a piece of grass from the ground we laid on. "You're asking the wrong person. I'm still new to all this."

"I think they prefer the night, or something like that," Autumn's small, melody voice quipped. "At least, that's what my friend October tells me. She said it makes her feel magikical, fresh, and so alive." She looked at me to see if I would agree or not.

I thought for a moment or two. The night did make me feel special, alive, and close to my inner vampire. Maybe October was right. I know in my point of view she is. "Yeah, that pretty much sums up how I feel once the grounds is covered in darkness. I like the daylight too, though. Is that strange? Like, when the sun is up I enjoy it and love the feeling of the sun on my skin. But once it's gone, I forget about it and enthrall in the darkness. The beauty of the moonlight, the moons, the blue pretty forest, the way everything seems to be alive but silent and watching."

Dylan looked at me in confusion. "You are a vampire? You don't smell like one," his voice was unsure. I laughed. So we have a smell like the werewolves do too. How interesting.

"Goddess, witch, and vampire," I dismissed the subject with my hand, trying to ignore his hanging jaw.

"Not just a witch, she's a witchan," Autumn exclaimed proudly. "She has silver blood," she whispered. Yeah, like someone would over hear-even though we were the only ones here.

"Impressive," he said in a odd tone. "I bleed blue," he added, laying onto his back, folding his arms up and under his head.

"Not fair! You guys have special blood and mine is just a normal red," Autumn pouted, crunching her face together.

We laughed at her expression. She really does want 'special blood'. "It's not cool being the freak. Your normal. I'm forever marked at a werido," I pointed out, easing her troubled mind.

Dylan shot me a look. "Your not a werido, or a freak. Besides, how do you know what your blood looks like? Have you checked it since you came here?" he turned to her, demanding.

She pondered in thought, pursuing her lips. "Noo, it's not something I really care to check."

"Your blood bleeds red, but it isn't blue in your veins. It's a strange blue mixed with

green," he said easily, making both mine and her mouth drop. "What?" he shifted nervously. "I can see people's blood. And see it-helloo, I'm a werewolf, remember?"
"I didn't know they could see our blood before its been shed," her face had paled. She looked like she was going to throw up. "How is that possible?"
I was curious about this myself, so I leaned in to hear his reply better. He laughed oddly, glancing at both of our's reactions. "Well, I don't know. Predator, right? Werewolves and witches and vampires were born separately, you know. Born to kill each other since the beginning of time. Like any other species, we all have gifts and whatnot to make the other weaker but equal. I can see your blood, smell it, change into a monster to attack. Witches are to be able to cast spells, some without even doing rituals called witchans. Vampires are strong as werewolves, but most are stronger, sharp teeth to cut through anything, and smart."
"What are their weaknesses?" He is smart, I noticed that quick enough. For someone as cute as him, it seemed impossible for them to also be intelligent.
He cleared his throat, sitting up. "Werewolves weakness is silver and spilled animal blood. Witches is that it takes them awhile to do a spell when they need it to be instant. Witchans are harder to break-but Witchlight should do the trick. Vampires that are allergic to the human realm sun is there weakness, but the others that are not, are. . let's say, a little weak when they smell spilled human blood."
He had my full attention. "And the Gods and Goddesses? What is their's?"
He smiled, showing sharp, long white teeth. I shivered looking at him. Shark teeth, but smaller. "Gods do not have a weakness, silly one. Only one thing-power. They strive for power, most wanting and needing it so bad it leads to their own undoing. Some even destroy their selves to get it. Like, Odin Omay. But you, you're unique. You have the best blood in you, so to speak honestly, that's why you pose a threat to everyone around you. Your nearly impossible to kill, Chlo'," he stole Autumn's nickname for me. Always leaving the E sound out of it.
"That's good to know," I replied in a dry voice. "Anything else, Einstein?"
He shrugged. "There's a lot more, too much just to say. Why, what do you want to know?"
Odin Omay. He had something about him losing power. Was that why he was here and not in Asgand?
"Odin, how did he lose power?"
He frowned, thinking hard. "He didn't lose power. He wanted it and received it. He went to Hades and they exchanged a oath or something similar to it. I don't know what for, nobody knows but Hades and Odin. It's illegal to found out, ya know. Forbidding. All I know is that he was a God first and served in mass wars before he was 22. During his time period, they had this draft for men-they had to be taken from their parents to join the military at six, to train them for when they turned 12. What they did was horrid, Chlo'. They whipped them daily, sometimes more than three times a day, sometimes starved them for long periods. Always fighting with swords to defend their own life.
"Odin was born a God, but it doesn't mean they cared nor that the hard life was any less painful. It just made him more tolerable, so they picked on him worse than the others. At 22, he had had enough. He was sick of killing, wars, fighting for his life. He went to

Hades, the underworld God, and asked for more than what he had. Hades agreed, making him join some kind of oath. Hades oath are always the worse, ya know. He can make you do whatever he wants, when he wants and you don't have a say in the matter. Your like a slave, a zombie without a soul or free will. Your will is his until the contract is over or when he says it is. So, Odin got what he wanted, I guess. I don't really know, I've never asked him about it and no one has dared to."

Hmm, good thing I like dares and is not afraid to be blunt and straight to the point. "Cool," I stated, trying to sound distant while everything inside of me was curious and wanted to know more. "How do you do a oath, anyhow?"

Autumn gasped, staring at me horrified. "Never, never do one!" Dylan yelled, his face twisted like her's. "I know your a Goddess, and how somewhere deep inside of you wants power, but no! You have to always fight that feeling, for the sake of losing your life or worse, your mind."

"Calm down. Jesus, I was just curious is all," I raised my hands. "I don't want any power. I'm content with this normal, safe life style." Did I just have bitterness in my voice? Do I really want to have all that?

His eyes narrowed at me, thinking. Whatever he saw in me made him decide to go on but hesitating. "This long, black and green stick. I forget the name of it. He mumbles something in ancient language, then grabs your wrist tightly," he grabbed mine, making me jump. His hands are warm and tight on my wrist. I felt the blood flow stop in them. "And then he whispers something again in the strange way of Gods. This odd, black thing shows under where his hand his. It moves and slithers like waves under the skin, permanently there for the rest of your life-and death." He let go of my hand, dropping it like I had burned him.

"I won't-I promise, I won't ever give an oath to anyone," I told him in the most serious, sincere voice I could. Autumn smiled weakly, taking my hand.

"You go all crazy on us and try to 'rule the world'?" I didn't answer, causing her to become paranoid. "Chloe, you have to promise you won't-"

"Stop it you two," I growled. "I don't think I'm going to try that one, I don't want power. But . . .I did have a vision of me in a war. I started it," I ducked my head so I couldn't see their reactions.

"Why-why the hell would you start a war?!" they both yelled at me. I felt even more worse then. I didn't want to-as of now-to start one. Hell, I didn't even know why I was going to!

"If you ever do, I'll be there for you. To help you win," Drake said, coming up the hill with his hands in his pockets. Dylan snarled, bringing his lips over his teeth, showing his gums. "Down, dog. I'm not here to start trouble. Yet," he added, smirking at him.

"Calm down, Dylan," Autumn laid her hand on his shoulder, his hated for the vampire instantly died out. Huh. I've never seen something like that before. With one touch and all his distaste and anger evaporated. Autumn is one strange creature, I thought, amused.

"Fine," he spat, not taking his eyes off of Drake as he sat next to me. If looks could kill ran threw my mind, making me shiver.

"How are you?" Drake whispered to me, not even looking at the other two, his eyes burning hotly into mine. Annoying butterflies fluttered throughout my stomach; I wanted to inch in closer to him and kiss him.

"I'm good," my voice higher than normal. He nodded, pleased I was okay. Hmm, I wonder what he is thinking? I closed my eyes and laid back on the grass. I didn't think of anything, didn't push his thoughts into mine. I felt him lay next to me and a second later he held my hand lightly, just so I could barely feel the heat coming off of his skin. 'She so beautiful, so exquisite, so special. Awh, crap. I'm screwed. She's has my heart already,' his pleasant thoughts made me smile. The way he saw me was enlightening. He saw me wrong, I was perfect in his eyes. Like I was an angel.

"What are you smiling about?" he asked, pulling me out of his thoughts.

I batted my eyelashes innocently at him. "Nothing." He grinned evilly-how I've come to adore that grin-. He was up to something, I know it. "What are you-Drake!" I yelled the last part, gasping when he placed himself between my legs, running his hands up and down my thighs.

"That is highly inappropriate," someone complained, but I didn't look or care to see who said it. Blood raced through my veins, my heart pounded at a 120 miles per hour. I was warm now, very warm. Drake's smile came slow and lustful as he looked down at me, his hands never leaving my body as they continued on their way up, bringing my dress up with them. I didn't want to, but I stopped him, placing my hands on his. No, let him! something screamed inside of me.

"Drake, we shouldn't," I pleaded for him to understand. His eyes remained intense for a few seconds longer before flashing to anger. He pulled his self away from me, looking else where but me. He was pissed, though he had absoutely no reason to be. Still, I couldn't help but feel guilty.

"Sorry," I muttered, lifting his chin to me so he would have no choice but to stare back. His eyes bore into mine, searching for something. I felt like he was trying to read into my soul, or he already had. He sighed, cupping my hand where it lingered on his cheek.

"Not your fault. I shouldn't touch what isn't mine," he grumbled. The way he said it made it sound like I belonged to someone already.

"You have my heart, until the next pretty boy comes along," I teased about the last part but I was serious of the first. He smiled weakly like he knew something I didn't. I raised my eyebrows at him, letting him know I was on to whatever he was hiding. He stuck his tongue out at me, letting me know he knew I knew and there was nothing I could do about it. "You're such a little kid."

He pushed me over lightly. "Yupp, and today I just turned 6!" he giggled, sounding much like a small child of six.

I rolled my eyes dramatically. "Your horrible. Where have you been all week?" I asked, turning more serious. I glanced over to where Autumn and Dylan was. They were leaning in to each other, whispering and laughing. Huh. They're hitting it off pretty well. Huh.

"No where," he looked away guilty. He's lying. People, especially the girls here, whisper more about Drake Malberry than any other guy, or girl for that matter.

He was always the hottest talk. Some claimed he had paid them nightly visit, only to get what he wanted then was gone the second it was over. Accordingly, he had slept with nearly every vampire female here, some even teachers!

"Visiting some girls, eh? Late hours?" I hinted, a little jealous. I didn't want him to sleep with girls. I wanted him to be my boyfriend and gladly become my boyfriend.

He grinned, looking at me again. "I only make a couple rounds daily. Trying to spread my talents around so that all the girls can share." I flinched, scooting away from him. Damned player. I should've known better than to like him. His easy looks and slick charms could fool any girl into there pants. Not this girl, I reminded myself. I won't let him do that so easy.

"That's great," I said threw closed teeth, trying to suppress a hiss. Had he thought I would give myself to him too? That I'd easily sleep with him and accept the fact he wasn't going to call on me anymore?

He grasped my hand. "Chlo'," why has every resorted to calling me that lately? "I don't want to hurt you. Not ever, if I can help it. 'Sides, I didn't think you like me. You never once hinted at it, only looked away when ever I complimented you or brushed your hair to the side."

I glazed hotly back into his eyes. "Of course I like you, you idiot. How has that not been visible to you? I-I just get really nervous around you and I don't know how to react to the things you say or do," I blurted stupidity. I've dated before and kissed, but never have I went farther than kissing, only one time and that was too painful to even think about.

"So, where does this leave us?" I asked, hoping he would ask.

He smiled. "Well, I'm not so sure. I've never dated a girl before, so how does this thing goes? Ahh, I think I got it. Chloe, will you be my girlfriend, to date me, a six year old boy? I promise if you say yes, I'd give you my squirt gun and a whole pack of gum," he held his hand up in scout's honor. I laughed, nodding my head.

"Fine, as long as I can sit next to you on the school bus and you share your pop rocks with me," I childishly replied. He laughed, wrapping his arms back around me. I rested my head comfortably on his chest, closing my eyes.

"Drake? Have you seriously never dated a girl?"

He cleared his throat. "Nahh, I never needed to when they so easily gave me what I needed. I've never felt this way about anyone, Chlo'. I knew you were special from the moment I saw you. I have a reputation to uphold, but it looks like you've destroyed it, my dear," he chuckled, pulling out a loose strand of hair and playing with it. "Your hair feels like silk, as every where else on you. I'd love to discover the rest of your body," he whispered into my ear, his lips brushing over my skin. I shivered at how good it felt. "In due time," he added.

I blushed, heat rising to my face. "What makes you think you're going to take that away from me?"

He looked at me with confusion written all over it. Then his face lightened, like a light bulb had gone off in his head. "Your a virgin? Impossible! Your too beautiful to be, I'm sure some man has snatched you up before." I didn't say anything, embarrassed. His lips settled on my forehead to kiss it there. "Don't worry. If and when the time comes, I'll be gentle. I am confident you will love me afterwards, like the other girls do."

He sounded so sincere, so promising. Could I trust him? From what I heard he is a player, never wanting to stay and be serious. But he wants me-does that mean he really likes me? I heard his thoughts, he never had a girlfriend. He's hiding something, something dark and sinister, I know that.

"Is there anything else you want to tell me?" I raised my eyebrows for empathize. I saw him gulp; he knows what I'm talking about. I followed his glaze to Autumn and Dylan. They were still wrapped in their own little world. At least they are hitting it off pretty well. Panic grew inside of me. They shouldn't be close already. I feared for my friends lives, that damned law.

"Yes," he replied slowly, his eyes still on them. "Later," he promised.

I nodded, turning my attention to them. "Hey, you two love birds."

Drake growled, I mean actually growled at that. "That's not possible," he spat, his hate for the werewolf was annoying. Why couldn't we couldn't get along like good little kids? I mused in my head.

"Shut up, you idiot. Anything is possible, its just a law not to. But, hey, if Chloe's parent's could-" Autumn began.

"And look up where they ended!" Drake snapped, making me flinch. "Sorry, but it's true." Autumn rolled her eyes dramatically, throwing his hands in the air before turning sharply to him. "He is just a friend. And if, if we decide to take it to that level, it's none of your damn business!"

Oh, god, that started Drake. His face became red with anger, resembling a Firecracker, his normally soft eyes cold and hatred.

"Okay, I think it's time to leave," I pulled Drake's arm, leading him back to the buildings. "Goodnight Autumn, Dylan. See you tomorrow," I said over my shoulder smiling. Once we were out of ear shot, I let Drake have it. "What the hell is your damn problem? I thought you wasn't bias against other species! Dylan's a good guy, so what's wrong?"

He stopped walking. We were in the garden. Even at night, it shined with beauty and smelled of roses, lavender, and so much more. "He's below us! Autumn is fine-a witch isn't so bad, but a goddamn werewolf? Are you insane, Chloe? You invited him to hang out with you? And the worst thing is you don't seem to be bothered at all by his presence!" he hissed. I had enough of the racism back in the human realm, and it seems no matter where you go there will always be prejudice.

"You better get used to it," I coldly replied, my voice sounding colder than ice. "He's going to be around for awhile. If you got a problem with him, then you can make some new friends. I can't date a bias guy." I turned on him and walked off in the other direction. I didn't take four steps before he caught my wrist and pulled me around to face him.

His lips crashed on mine, immediately sending flashes of fire throughout. Oh, God, how does he have this effect on me? His hands crept up and around to cup my butt, pulling up in the air and slamming me against the wall. A moan escaped my lips, I fingered his hair, pulling tightly on the strands, his mouth opened and gasped.

I felt his tongue traveling the area of my neck, sending chills in me. With my legs wrapped around his waist I could see and feel his penis poking through his pants, waiting to claim me.

Someone cleared their throat loudly, to let us know he or she was there. Drake sighed, pressing his forehead against mine before setting me back on my feet. Very casually he placed his arm around my waist and pulled me close to him.

"Hello, Odin." I suppressed a horrified gasp, swallowing nervously. He was standing not three feet away from us, his stone-but beautiful-face emotionless as always.

Odin glared silently at me, then Drake and then back to me. "Hello, you two. Nice little show you had there," he gave a stressed chuckle.

Drake grinned, acting like Odin was a long time friend and he could anything or act any way around him. "Yeah, maybe you should've came a little later and then it would of been a great show for you to watch. How long have you been there staring before you announced yourself?" he spat. Jesus, does he not have any respect for anyone?! How casually he could stand there and glare hatefully at a God!

His death will certainly result from his sharp mouth, watch. He's going to cross the wrong person one day and their going to snap.

Odin laughed; he knew this wasn't a fair fight-he could easily wipe him out . . . with his sharp words or moves. "Ay, long enough to know you've broken a school rule and should be suspended or expelled. Luckily, I feel like being nice tonight," he added, I released air from my lungs. I hadn't even know I was holding my breath. "So, you have another victim to make out with tonight, eh? Pity, the last five from yesterday will be so disappointed." Drake hissed, stepping forward to him. "You little-"

"Drake!" I snapped, angry he would dare yell at Odin. "Shut the hell up, you idiot." I didn't like seeing Drake hiss at him, or anyone to yell at Odin. Great. I need to seriously get over these strong, overbearing emotion I have for the God\/Vampire. Staring at him, I knew it was a hopeless cause-I'd love him till the day I die. Sad, I know. He doesn't even look at me in that kind of way and secondly, I already liked him a lot from the second I first laid eyes on him. How disgusted and ashamed I am of myself right now. My eyes averted from him and looked at something more safe, the rose bush near us.

"You need to watch what you say, boy. One day I won't be able to control my temper and you'll suffer from it, not me," his voice turned to that of a true God. It radiated from power, command, and oblivious authority. I was scared, never had I heard a more terrifying tone. I shrinked back into the wall, noticing Drake did the same.

"I'm sorry," he whispered, not liking he had to be defeated and scared of him.

Odin ignored him with a slight nod to let him know he had heard him. "Chloe," he said in a softer voice, "you never showed for your training this week. Would you like to start now? No pressure, you can do it tomorrow."

Spend time with him? Hell yeah I'm willing to go now! Anything to be around him a second long. Odin smiled. "Ahh, your mind is amusing to me, Favatte," he said the last part in a strange language. I don't know why, but I blushed, knowing whatever he added in the ancient language it was referring to me. Only problem was what did it mean? Drake didn't find this amusing as I did.

"What did you just call her? Repeat it in English," he hissed, looking back and forth to me and Odin. He suspected we were keeping secrets, when it I don't even know anything but English.

Odin's eyes narrowed, turning black as he glared at the young fool next to me. "None of your business. Are you coming or not?" he asked me politely in a quiet, sweet voice. What was that other tone? Something I couldn't figure out or begin to understand.

"Okay. See you later?" I gave Drake my best pleaded eyes, begging him to reason with me. I wanted to be with Odin more than anything, but that didn't mean I didn't like Drake. How couldn't I, when he is so dangerous and sexy?

His lips twitched, he wasn't happy with me. I sighed, I have a lot to make up for him, and we just started dating. "Okay, go. Wait," he called when I began to walk to Odin. He pulled me into his arms and kissed me fully on the lips, I met him with passion for passion. I know I should've cared that someone was watching us-Odin at that!-but with Drake, I couldn't care less. I wanted him, I love how he easily makes my heart pound and make it feel like its going to bust at any second. "See you later," he added seduce-ivy. Yeah, I'm a nerd even in my head. I like to make up my own words and separate them as they sound.

"Okay," I breathlessly replied, reluctant to leave his arms. I backed away, my head bowed, as I walked over to Odin. I was mad at myself how I threw my self at him willingly when he kissed me, out in public. I have to stay at a good distance away whenever I'm around Drake.

"We're going to transport," Odin snatched my arm then let it go just as fast as he had taken it. We were inside of some empty gym, or what looked like a gym. Only this one has a much higher ceiling and instead of the fake wooden floors, it was a odd purple-black.

"It's called Glarpy. It's a type of floor made from Faeries so that we can train and you wouldn't hurt yourself from hitting the ground too hard. Think of it as a mat, only softer." My hand blindly lean down to touch it. It felt like any other floor, just as hard and solid. "Like most Faerie made things, it is much more than it appears. Haven't you ever heard looks are deceiving?" he threw a sword to me. Acting on impulse, I caught it by the handle.

"It's . . ." I struggle with a word to describe the sword. It was brilliant, bright but dark colors of purple and blue. The purple looked to have a little bit of black in it, and another color I've never seen before. Green and yellow revealed itself in it when I tilted it to different sides, the light catching the hidden colors only every once in a while. The handle itself was carved like a J with swirls and ancient writings on it. The blade flashed millions of different colors and shades, never wanting to settle on a color, it seemed. The blade is sharp, looking sharp enough to cut through metal, brick, and everything else.

"Indescribable, I know. It's an old sword of mine, I used it back in the B.C.'s, maybe before that. It's very valuable today," he shrugged, not caring of its worth. His own sword was magnificent! Bright colors of red, yellow, orange, green, and blue with designs only he could translate.

"I can't use this," I whispered hoarsely. "It's too unique and precious to you, and I'm sure to the entire world." I tried to hand it back to him, but he shook his head, refusing to give it back.

"Once it lays in someone else's hands, you cannot give it back to the old owner. It is your's now. And to answer your question in your mind, yes, I just made that rule up," he laughed, infuriating me more. "Now, be serious, Chloe. I have to train you and we have a lot to go over, so let's begin."

I was irate at him, but he still refused to take it back. The three hours with him flew by fast, much to my disappointment. He worked me to the bone and more, correcting my every move, breathe, blinking I made.

"No, no, separate your legs like this." He lightly spread my legs apart, not careful as to where his hand went. I blushed, of course, my heart reacting to his touched. But I was his puppet, his student and touching me didn't thrill him. Or at least from the emotionless look in his eyes, that's what it told me. Then again, he is experienced in hiding his true feelings. Gah, I hate being so confused!

On and on we went, he corrected me from the way I breath to the way I look! "Is this even important?" I snapped, furious at his remarks.

"Everything is important when it comes to defending yourself! Stop talking, do as I say and listen," he snapped right back. He was impossibly fast, knocking me to my feet at least three dozen times before he finally said our session was over. He looked normal, like he hadn't even moved. I, on the other hand, is covered in sweat. My muscles are screaming for rest and a long, hot, relaxing bath to sit in and fall asleep for a week.

"You did excellent for your first time," he finally smiled at me. Throughout the whole freaking three hours he didn't crack a smile or anything, always the stoned face! But how perfect that stone face is, like a statue brought to life.

"Yeah, right," I stated sarcastically. He yelled at me too much for me to be good, screamed at me was more like it. Oh, I groaned mentally, I want to lay down or sit for a month and never get up! I pictured myself in the morning, how sore I'll be by then. Thank goodness we have a four day weekend. I'm going to need those four days to recover from all the techniques and moves he taught me. Seriously, I would've thought he was teaching me martial arts not this, if it wasn't for the heavy sword in my hand the whole time.

He chuckled lightly. Ohh, he's in a good mood. Ugh, I never knew he took joy from other people's discomfort and pain. That's nice to know now, sick, beautiful, mean, kind, demanding God.

"Chloe, I've never seen someone move so quickly the way you did on your first day in training, most don't even move like that after their tenth session! You have you're fathers blood, no doubt. He was an excellent ninja, one of the best our world has ever seen. For a moment there, I thought we traveled back in time and I was training him and not you. I can't wait to see how you are as the session progress into months," he clapped his hands excitedly.

Months? Man, what the hell did I get myself into? He's going to drain me! I don't think I can survive another session with him and his teachings. "You'll survive. Of course your sore now, but you won't be in the morning or ever again, I promise. Your Vampire and Goddess blood allows you to handle this more and be better in it, that's why you are going to be such a good assassin. Already you move like a person of much training. From here on out, it'll get better," he promised, helping me to my feet. "Do you want a transport to your room?" he asked, clearly amused with all this. Damn him to hell!

"Yes," I muttered weakly. I need something-I don't know what, but whatever it is I need it badly and now. My body ached and called for whatever it is, pleaded with me to get it. I don't know what you want! Just tell me! I yelled back at it. This is crazy-my body is craving something I don't even know what. I must be losing my mind.

I looked up to see we were in my apartment. "Thanks." I made my way to the couch and collapsed on it, closing my eyes. I need . . . I need . . .Dammit, what the hell do I need?!

I suddenly smelled an overly sweet and empowering scent. I breathed in longer, deeper-trying to enclose myself with the odd, but amazing smell. My body screamed for that smell, my throat grew drier, burning my nostrils and throat. "Here," Odin said. I opened my eyes to see him holding a glass filled with dark red liquid. I blindly took it, not thinking, and sipped at it. My eyes grew wide, my eyes dilated, my pores literally felt like they were opening. I gulped the rest down eagerly, wanting to devour the sweet taste. It was like wine only much, much, much more better in tasting, gave you a higher buzz and a better one. I wanted more instantly, wanted at least a keg of the red dark liquid he gave me.

"Mmm," I moaned, licking the rim of the glass. "What was that?" In my drunken state, Odin looked far more beautiful. I wanted him more at that moment more than anything in my life. I would do anything to have him, just for a minute even. Okay, not in that kind of perverted way-more like in a killing spree, oath-binding, sick way.

He smirked, hearing my thoughts. "Blood, human to be specific. Don't give me that horrified look, Chloe, it's okay for you to drink it. You are half vampire," he casually stated. Half, what the hell? "Yes, half. You won't be a full vampire until your mentor changes you, which is me or whoever it appointed to you if you are to change mentors. Still, you're different, so it doesn't surprise me that you already crave human blood."

I nodded, taking all this in. Funny thing is, I'm not ashamed. I only wanted more, my body and mind demands it. "Can I-" I didn't even have to finish before he handed me another glass. Where did that come from? Crap, I don't care as long as I have it.

I slowly took it, wanting to smell it longer, remember the lovely scent to it. This one smells stronger, it has to be from a different human, I am convinced of that. Ever so slowly, I taste the sweet blood, enthralled with it completely. Too soon it was gone again, I want more but I know I should stop here.

My body feels normal again, the soreness that started to creep in faded away. Replaced it was the need to stare and taste Odin. Please, please leave before I lose my self control, I said in my head knowing he would hear it.

The bone head ignored my plea, only smiling in delight for some twisted reason. "You know, you are going to be the strongest Vampire I've never had the pleasure of meeting and in all history, for that matter. Ah, besides me, of course. No half vampire could resist the smell, the taste the way you just did. Not to mention your very essence demanded, needed more and yet, you told yourself 'no more' and you pushed the need back. You are something else, Chloe," he shook his head in admiration.

I smile smugly. "I know," I chimed. "Your beautiful, you know that?" I blurt. He blushes, actually blushes. Finally! I found a soft spot in his stone-like expression! I grin, happy he really is self conscious. Who would've thought this man would think he isn't? He easily is the definition of beautiful without over doing it. No one is perfect, but he is pretty damn close to it.

"Stop it. I'm not beautiful, and anyways isn't that a term to describe a woman not a man?" he looked away, the blood still rushed to his cheeks.

"It's easier for a woman to be beautiful, still hard nevertheless. But to call a man that, it means he is beautiful inside and out, and is much more rare for a man to be called that. You are beautiful," I replied, my voice velvet smooth and low. I rose to my feet, standing only inches from him. His body trembled, looking down at the ground. "Your personality, your face, your body, your smell coming from your skin, everything that makes you is striking, stunning, amazing." I reached out to touch his face but stopped and let it drop to my side. As much as I want to touch him, I wouldn't do so without his approval. God help me, I think I'm hopelessly in love.

"You think too highly of me," was all he said sadly. "If only you knew of my past, my haunting dreams, my-" he cut himself short.

"Tell me, Odin. I don't think you could of ever done anything horrid. What is it that makes you so disgusted with yourself and shuts you off to the world? You can't deny it! You talk to people, yes. I've seen you though, you hide your true emotions behind a mask, you never touch anyone unless you have to, and you live here not in Ashgand. What troubles you?"

He pulled up his sleeve on his left arm, turning his wrist so I could see-my god! It was what Dylan claimed he has! Words didn't do justice, not even close. The black thing under his skin moves like a wave, where it showed a second before it disappears the next and reappears in another area-all within three inches-then disappears again and goes back to the original spot it was at only to start the process all over. I couldn't take my eyes off of it. It screamed nothing but evil, sinister, and lethal. What disturbed me the most is something about it reminds me of Drake. Please, let that just be a grudge and not a gut instinct.

I place my hand on it, finding it ice cold. I release air from my lungs and it showed in the air. Impulsively, I back away from the evil thing forever marked on him, even in death.

"What did he make you do?" I'm scared to death to even ask, but I have to know. I want to help Odin, help take some of his pain from him. Dylan said it was a classified subject so no one ever knew, and I'm his student specifically. He would tell me more than anyone else. I hope so, anyways.

"Horrible, monstrous, demon-like things," he laughs bitterly, his eyes turning to black. No, I want his soft, green blue eyes back. This isn't the man I think I love. "The worse history has ever know, thank goodness that they covered the my tracks for me, and the mess. Trust me, your innocent mind doesn't want or need to know. Your visions may allow you see the details, and I don't want that to happen. I enjoy the fact you think so highly of me," his hand brushed my hair back that hand fallen in front of eyes. "Your boyfriend has fallen asleep in his room. You should go to bed too." He turned to my door, pausing at it. "Goodnight, Chloe. Thanks for the pleasant conversation. I rather find it amusing and relaxing."

"Goodnight, my lord," yeesh, how it still makes me embarrassed to call him that, "sweet dreams. I mean it. And the feeling is mutual, thanks for listening to the babbling I had to say." I yawned, the high I felt from the drink still lingering in on me. Blood does a strange thing to Vampires-it heightens their senses, makes them stronger. Well, I know from class that half Vampires that is what happens. When we change, we are automatically strong and all that. All the half Vampires and full Vampires will change and already had on their own. They bodies do it, something with the blood or whatever. I'm the last in many, many years that will require a good ole sucking on the neck. I giggle at that aloud.

Vampires can change someone, but it is illegal without approval from a Elder or a Consile. Vampires can make their venom come at will, but like I said, its illegal and if you disobey it the consequences are exile or death. But people like me and Odin-people that have Goddess and God blood-can change someone whenever we want, when we please to. Not to mention the chances of surviving a bite from one of us is more likely than that of a normal Vampire. Interesting, very. And the victim that we change will be tied to us, it can be sexual, emotional or anything. Sometimes they also receive our talents, not as strong, but still. It's something, right? When you have nothing you appreciate what little you get? Personally, I can't wait to get bit from Odin. I hear its very pleasant just for a Vampire to bit you-so imagine being changed by him. My heart pounded at the thought.

I bet his blood taste good-wait, does a Vampire drinking from another Vampire blood even taste good?-he smells good enough, hypnotic like blood. I smile at that thought. I had originally believed blood wouldn't taste so good, now I've changed my opinions greatly. It was the best beverage ever. Now I know how most people here think of humans so lowly. If they were to think of them as normal then they couldn't drink from them, control them, and so much more the dirty things they do to humans.

I tuck my arms under my head, smiling with my eyes closed. Haha, even Vampires are not true Immortals. Only half Immortal. Gods and Goddess are truly Immortal-that's why I'm such a threat to this world and every other world ever made. In all, there are Nine Worlds. Scary to think there are so many.

Personally, I love it here. Not because of the people-most of the girls give me dirty looks, don't know why-but because of the beauty and the smells and the feeling of feeling complete here.

"Whatcha thinking about?" Drake's voice made me open my eyes in shock.

"How the hell do you keep getting through my apartment? I know the last two times I had the door locked." I squinted my eyes at him. I don't want to have to read his mind. I know how aggravating and disrespectful that is but if he doesn't tell me soon, I'm going to have to and call him out.

He grinned, sitting next to me on the couch. "Well, I can go through walls. Happy? I know you're hiding something to me too. So spite it out already. What is it?" The look on his face told me he already knows. Damn him.

"I can read minds and I have visions. Now, what about you? Don't you have something to admit to me, too?" I lean in closer to him. Earlier he told me he would tell me later. It is later now.

His grin instantly disappears, replacing it is a cold, dispatched glare. "Would you be surprised is I told you my father is pure evil?"

I laughed, throwing my head back. That's it? I thought it would be something unforgivable, something that would make me wish I had never asked in the first place. "I guess?"

"Do not take me so lightly," he retorted. "I'm serious. His name is Lucifer, you know, the devil. Funny thing is, he has heard of you and how close we've become. He has requested us to come to his house tomorrow, for dinner. In a normal situation, I would tell him hell no, but you can't deny what he wants," he sighed heavily. "We have to go, I'm so sorry Chloe. You know, I changed my name when I moved here? It was Christopher, get it? It's like Lucifer . . .and I don't want any ties to him. At all. He's not that bad, if you don't cross him. But other than, you will be safe," he promised me. Who was he trying to reassure, him or me? I don't want to go, but what other choice do I have?

"I'll go. If he tries anything.." I warned.

"No, no. He wouldn't dare-you're Odin's student. I think he is curious of your heritage more than anything. It's formal dressing, so you should probably wear a dress. Something dark, or red. He loves red on a woman," he hinted to me. I am not wear the most commonly know as a 'whore colored' dress. I have three types of dresses-two boring and bland dresses. One that is ordinary and pretty enough, long to the ankles. And four other, very special dresses-mostly coming up to the knees, tight, low cut, dark colors, and absolutely gorgeous. Hmm, I think one of those will do.

"Okay. I have a dress already picked out," I grinned, evilly.

He didn't catch onto the double lines. He just nodded silently. "That's fine. Dinner is at 6, since it takes three hours to transport there (for the most bizarre reason) we will leave at 2. Is that agreeable with you?"

Chapter Three: Dinner with the Devil

My eyes flew open. I groan out loud. Great. Today I have to go meet Drake's father. Dinner with the devil, I thought, slightly amused and terrified. He wants to meet the freak? Fine, a freak he will met. Haha. Jesus, why does my hair have didn't hair textures on different days? Why can't it just stick with one? I stupidly asked my self while staring in the mirror. At least today it is nearly straight with waves in all the right place. That's one thing off the to-do list. Not bothering to brush it out, I applied purple and blue eye shadow to my eyes, blending it perfectly. After that, I put black eyeliner on under my eyes and at the tips of my eye lids, making my eyes look larger and prettier. Satisfied with the way things are going, I moved on to a light color lipstick. Vampires have excellent complexions, so I don't have to worry at all about foundation or blush.

After doing my eyelashes and curling them up, I went to my closet to pull out my favorite dress. It came about a inch above my knees and was tight around the breast and stomach, showing off my figure amazingly. It is a deep blue, with a low cut cleavage, no sleeves-thank effing God-but straps. When I first saw it, a few months ago, I had fallen in love with. Just looking at it made me squeal in delight as I ran my hands lightly over it. It feels better than silk and velvet. I put it on, loving how it lifts my breast and make my legs look shapely, my stomach flat, and my buttocks firm and round. The shoes are jet blue and three and a half inches tall, with raw cut diamonds near my toes. It fits my dress accordingly.

Maybe I should wear my hair up? I thought as I glanced at myself in the full body mirror. No, it is fine, I told myself. You look fairly descent, I think Drake will be proud to call you his girlfriend. Nodding to my self, I spray some perfume on. Just enough to give a light scent. Ugh, I can't stand people that seems to spray the whole bottle on them and you can smell them five minutes before they enter the room. Seriously people, do you stink that bad or what?

"My God," someone sharply took a breath in. I smiled, knowing it is Drake without looking up. "You were beautiful before . . .You are stunning even more so! Chloe, I didn't think you could ever look more gorgeous, but yet again you prove me wrong," his eyes slowly trail over my body, doing it three times before sighing. "My father is going to love you." What that bitterness or something else? I couldn't tell.

"Thank you. You look sexy yourself," I grin, giving him a once over. His silver eyes are twinkling with mischief, full of life and love. He is wearing dark blue blues, designer jeans no doubt from the looks of them, with a perfectly cut in them. Strangely, he has on a tux jacket but instead of a button down shirt underneath it is a white, plain shirt. To top it off, his feet are covered with Chucks. I had to admit even with the odd but sexy outfit, he looks so handsome. Oh, the hearts he must've of broken! Those pink, full lips turned up just enough to tease you and make you want to kiss him. Those twinkling eyes of his, taunting you, daring you to do it.

He steps up next to me in front of the mirror, pulling me tight against his body. His cologne, oh how to ever explain the sweet, masculine smell? It was appealing to me too much as I breathed in deeper, noticing how his heart beat sped up. "We look amazing together," he nibbled in my ear, goose bumps betraying me and showing on my arms. He's right. In my heels, he is a inch tall than me, still. My hair, my face, my body complimented his. Hell, we look more than just amazing together. I smiled with pride, watching his face as his eyes drupe in the most sexy way, making him look like he was seducing me. My arms reached up and around me to cradle his neck. His head lowered to mine, his lips near mine.

Sharply, he pulls away with a teasing smile. Damn him! I hope his father is not as teasing as he is! Grasping my hand, he pulls me close to him again. "Close your eyes," he commanded, sounding afraid. "You do not want to see what we are going to pass through. It his transport," he sneers 'his'. "Its terrifying to see, let alone hear." I close my eyes and feel air ruffling and whipping my hair all around.

"Prettyy, little girl. You smell good. Wonder what it would taste like to bite through that living skin," a horrible voice hiss. Screaming, horrifying, anguishing voice loom around me, closely. I press my head into Drake's chest, trying to miserably block them out.

"Where am I?" another cried, confused and scared. "Chloeee," one whisperers evilly.

"You know," Drake said in a shaking voice, "I've never seen a more beautiful woman as you in my life. You are amazing." He was trying to coax me, to calm me. Well, it was working.

"Liar," I accuse. He has many girls before, pretty I'm sure. There was no way in heck he was telling the truth.

"I'm telling you the truth. Read my mind and you will see that," he stated seriously. The voice began to fade into the background. I reached up to wrap my arms around his neck, not wanting to invade his privacy. We stood there silently, holding the other tightly. It was incredible, to feel the emotions he was having for me, the smell of him, the hold he has on me. "Open your eyes. We are here."

"It's pretty," I gasp, for it is pretty. Dark and lowly lit, but pretty in it's own way.

"Ay, that you are," he chuckled, kissing me on the forehead dearly. I felt him stiffen before he pulled away, his eyes glaring coldly behind me. "Hello, Father," he flatly said.

"I haven't seen you in years and this is how you say hello? Oh, Drake, you were always such a moody one," came a teasing, velvety voice. My body reacted strangely then, my heart racing just hearing the stranger, my knees growing weak and light.

I turn around slowly. I should've been prepared, should've done something. But who could've known his father would be even more sexy than him? His hair is silver-black, like his son, only his eyes are silver-blue, so oddly familiar. I thought Drake had eyes filled with twinkling mischief, nothing could compare to his father's lively, bright ones. They captured me, taunted me, begged me to come closer to him. As his bore into mine I saw clear passion, lust . . .and love? He was taller than Drake, and more muscular. His face reminded me of Odin's-not that they look the same-but because of the beauty they easily seem to possess. Odin's features are beautiful, sweet, while Luce's (I refuse to call him Lucifer. He does not look like a Devil) is sexy, sleek, charming.

I watch as Luce's eyes roam of my body many times, stopping in all the 'right' places. His smile came slow, taunting me even more, his eyes intense, sending butterflies in my stomach. I finally understand what people mean when someone is undressing them with their eyes. If Drake wasn't here, I am positive he would try to take me to bed. His hands are long and strong, how would they feel touching every inch of my body? Those full lips would be mind-blowing, I am sure of it. They way he held his body told me how slick, smooth, and womanizing he really is. The hell-no pun intended-if he is. I want him.

Slowly, careful not to shock me, he grabs my hand and bows to me, his eyes boring into mine. "Lakota, is it?" he mummers. I only nod, speechless for once. He kisses my hand, lingering on him. For a split second I felt his tongue lick over my hand, forcing me suppress a moan. My heart skips a beat, literally. Once it started again, I wince at the pain that fills my chest. "Mm, you okay, love?" His easily, confident grin tells me he knows my heart skipped.

"I am fine. Shouldn't we . . ?" I left unfinished. They both nod, not looking at the other. Yeesh, what is their problem with each other? Men!

"Yes, of course. Drake," he placed his hand out in the opposite direction for him to proceed.

Dinner would've been pleasant, if Luce hadn't been staring hotly at me the whole time! Whenever I spoke or he was he had his eyes glued to me, never leaving my face as if he wanted to remember every detail of my face, my body, my voice. I did the same, though. I know. I shouldn't have, but how can you help it when someone so sexy, young looking, and charming averts his whole attention to you?

"Dammit," Drake suddenly growls, banging his fists on the table. "I am sorry, Chloe. I have to leave; I am getting the feeling Odin wants to talk to me. I will return shortly, soon, for Odin's transporting is much, much quicker."

I place my finger on his lips to silence his words. He seemed so troubled, so angry at something. He closed his eyes, kissing my finger. "Go, Drake. Tell Odin I will be there to see him on scheduled time."

He rose to his feet, kissing my forehead before turning to glare hatefully at Luce. Then, he disappeared. Now what am I to do? I am stuck here, alone with Luce. This not going to be good.

"Sapphire," he calls to me, standing only a feet away. I felt my body respond eerily to the name he calls me, the hair on the back of my neck standing straight up. My body boiling over with the sudden need I have for him. "Tell me, what is you're relationship with Odin, my sapphire?" I shiver again at his velvety smooth voice.

Stupidly I look up to meet his eyes. What had he meant? His attitude suggested like there would be something more. "He is my lord, my mentor, Luce. Nothing more," I added, a little bitterly.

He gave a low hiss. "You like him, but he is blind to what you feel. That's not right, sapphire. He should see you like the woman you are. You-"

I look away nervously. "Stop calling me sapphire."

He laughs, sitting on the table in front of me. "You like me calling you sapphire. I can see it, the way your body reacts to it like its heard it before. Ahh, now, be serious. Who is this Lee Mortenson?" he innocently asks.

I gasped, covering my hand with my mouth. That's how his eyes look so familiar! Lee Mortenson! He was my old neighbor before he moved to supposedly Washington. I-to put it nicely, he and I had sex. Lee was my first and only, I haven't had sex since. But it was more than just sex, the way he had moved in bed was as if he was making love to me. Slow, passionate, then building to we couldn't control it anymore and- "You can't be him. Your eyes are the same, nothing else." I knew it was a lie when I uttered it.

His hand reached out to my face, his index finger tracing my lip as I closed my eyes, remembering how great it was. "I am him. I can change my appearances. I can prove it to you, but honestly, I think showing you will be so much more fun," he whispered, his voice seducing again.

I pushed it hand away. That was in the past, not now! The now is where I am dating his son. Doesn't he care about that? Nope, I answered myself. You saw how they act around each other, he doesn't care. "You shouldn't-we shouldn't. It isn't right!" I yell at the man, though my body craves for his.

"I don't care if is right or not. I want you, and that is the end. Besides, my love, we haven't done anything. Yet," he added, hinting at double lines.

"And we won't!" I screamed back. God, Drake, where the hell are you? Hurry back, my boyfriend.

Suddenly he hisses, rising to his feet. "Damn phone. That's why I never wanted one in the first place."

He slammed the door after him, the phone ringing stopped as he must've answered it.

Two minutes later he reappeared, looking confused and a little joyful. "Drake called. He said that you won't be returning tonight. All, every single one, of the portals are closed. They are looking into it. Until then, you will be staying here. I am truly sorry." I would've believed him, if his body and face didn't show how happy he was. Oh, just my effing luck. I'm stuck here, in the underworld, with the devil I already slept with. Did I mention he is my boyfriends father? I thought bitterly.

"Show me my room. I want to go to bed," I sharply snap at him. The fewer the seconds I have to spend with him and his charming ways, the safer I will be.

"Go to bed? Why, sapphire, I was hoping we would have some fun." His grin was back; I don't know what he wants but I need to get out of here. Quick. I will be powerless in his arms, and not because he would force me . . .No, it would be my own doing.

"Show. Me. My. Bedroom," I hiss through my teeth, they were clinched tightly. He's pissing me off. I don't want to have 'fun.' I have a pretty bright vision what his fun would be.

"Be calm, my love. I was only teasing you," he shook his head smiling. "Come," he held his hand out, but I ignore it, walking beside him down the long hallway.

"What the fuck?" I snarl, noticing a picture through open doors. I stop to get a closer look at it, making sure it is what I thought. Yupp, that is me. I was wearing strange clothing, from another time period. My body was pressed against his, his hands wrapped around my body. His lips were at my neck, his eyes low as mine. "You have a painting of me and you?"

His smile is slow and smug as he looks at the painting of me and him. "That's not you. Notice the date on it, silly girl. It was you, just before you were reborn."

I turn sharply, not wanting to look at the picture. I cross my hands over my chest. "Excuse me? That cannot be me, I didn't pose for it or anything. I don't even remember being with you in your normal appearance. Heck, we were only together one time. Besides, what the hell makes you think I'll do it again? So you can wipe that smug grin off your face." In a flash he covers the distance between us, he was so close I had no choice but to back into the wall, shrinking as I read his lust in his body and eyes. Though his face was angry.

"I believe you will, many times over and over again. As long as Odin doesn't get in the way, again. That is you, you just don't remember. Yet. You will, when you come into age, that's how reborn Immortals are. They don't really remember their past lives until they reach the age of 18. Wanna hear a story, Sapphire?" he whispers into my ear, his eyes slowly glazing over my body.

"No," I manage to choke out, unable to say anything else. I do want to hear the story, though my body told me to run, to ignore the words he is about to say. For it would be the truth, the cold hearted truth I need to hear but would be painful for me in the long run.

"Some how, I think you do. See, once a upon a time there was this mortal named Sonya. Oh, she was beautiful, many men courted her, including immortals, even Odin himself. Me and him, well, we were once very close friends, almost like brothers. He fought in wars beside me, as I did to him. He wrote to me, saying how he met this perfect, charming woman-only problem was she was a human. Illegal even then, to even him. I moved in with them, after I lost my house-don't ask why-and withdrew from the wars they made me fight in. Odin never did, he loved it, fighting and killing people.

"I met her, his Sonya. I was fascinated by the way she walked, talked, held her head, even the way she looked lovingly at Odin whenever he was near. Of course, he wasn't always there, being drafted into wars and all, but I tried being a good friend. Really, I did. It was just so hard. She didn't know it, but her eyes tempted me, begged me to love her when Odin was away. So, I started to advance on her, knowing she would refuse me but I did so anyways. She did, for a long time, until she became lonely from Odin being gone so much. One night when I tried to kiss her, she didn't push me away, instead she grabbed me hard and pulled me against her. Oh, how I loved her, she alone held my heart forever and always." He leans in closer to me, his lips only a inch away now.

"I knew she didn't want or love me, I was just her plaything until he came back. Then the nights and days belonged to him and she would ignore me. She loved him too much, as he did her, I could see it. Just by the way they looked at each other. I was filled with hate and jealousy-I wanted her to be mine! Not to make love to him anymore! But noo, she wanted him . . .andd eventually me too. She became confused, not knowing which to choose; me or him? She would cry often, begging for me to understand, to give her more time until she decided which man she wanted. I would of never left her, even if she were to chose him! Then she told him the truth-how I loved her, she loved me, and how we had been sneaking behind his back. He forgave HER, but set out to destroy me!

"Around that time, he hired some guys to kill me, so she wouldn't know it was him. Only, she got in the way of the killing. When they came after me, she saw what was about to happen and threw herself in front of me right before the knife could go through my stomach. My sapphire, it was horrible watching you die. You died in order so I would live," he cried, bowing his head on my shoulder. "Watching the life drain out of you, you touched my cheek and smiled faintly before you closed your eyes. I wanted to kill Odin then, but I left instead, how could I kill him knowing you still enjoyed his company? I couldn't do it, even after your death."

I lightly place my hand on his head, soothing him. This did make sense, the nickname he calls me-I've heard it before. Only a long time ago. The way he looks at me, the way I feel in return, I felt it all before. "But me and Odin does not have that kind of relationship," I mutter stupidly, not knowing what else to say to him.

His body stiffen straight up. "Ahh, but you will. I know him well, my love. He wants to do things differently, try to stay away from you and your allure. He will not succeed, I am positive. Do not let him touch you! You are mine! You belong to me, before my damned son, or any other men for that matter! I claimed you while you were young, took you and loved you for only one day, still you are mine. I will not let some idiotic, foolish young man take you from me," he hiss, bringing his face close back to mine.

"No, Luce, don't. That was in the past. I am dating your son, please," I beg, knowing it was hopeless. He will have what he wants, and so will I, no matter how much my thoughts deny and fight it. My body wants his, my soul wants his. I could feel it pulsing threw my veins, ready to take over the minute he kisses or touches me.

His hand reaches out to caress my cheek, my neck, then settling on my breast. I could hear how jagged his breath already is, how mine already is. "I couldn't care less if you were dating the King of the world or anything like it. You are mine," he hisses again, impulsively pressing his lips on mine. I gasp, opening my mouth to let his tongue in. His passion before was no match for what it is now, he had been holding back before. This time, he demanded more, his lips working over mine fastly, wanting to claim me again. I manage to pull away, only it didn't stop him. His lips move on toward my neck, giving long, wet kisses to them. Unwillingly, a moan escapes my mouth, before I try to push him away. "Luce, we shouldn't. I don't want-"

He moans, setting his hands on my waist before grinding them against his. "Mm, you don't want what? This?" his hands roam underneath my shirt, playing with my nipples. My knees grow weak, feeling like dough. "Or this?" his head ducks as he pulls up my shirt, exposing my breast. His teeth bite gently on my nipples, making them instantly grow hard. "Or this-"

"Quit, Lucifer!" I snap, shoving him hard against the wall across from us. "I told you, we shouldn't." I look up into his eyes, a huge mistake. The passion, the lust, the love he has for me is unbearable to see. My lips press back to his, meeting this time passion for passion.

"Let's go to my room," he slyly tells me, his hands roaming all over my body, bringing the dress with his hands as he brought it up. I didn't say yes, but I didn't say no either. He took my silence as an okay and scooped me up in his arms. His lips never left mine, they stayed on me like he was hot glue. I barely felt it when he lowered me to his bed, only the softness of the satin covers touching my naked skin. Naked? No, I have to get hold of myself before this goes too far. Remember Drake, Chloe, a voice demands some where deep inside of me. I don't want to. I don't want this feeling to ever end.

I push the voice out of my mind, becoming deeper into kissing Luce. I open my eyes to see him smiling down at me before I rip his shirt off of him, revealing a nicely defined chest-okay, nice is a weak word for his body. Sexy is more like it. My hands reach out to touch his chest, running over his nipples and biceps and stomach, ecstatic how strong he is yet smooth and soft like a young man would feel like.

"Your killing me with your thoughts and hands," he moans, dipping his head low to kiss my neck. His hands open my legs for him to fit easily in them, touching every inch of my legs, going up all the way until he had my dress over my head and flung it to the floor. I grin evilly, unbuttoning his pants and taking him into my hands with long, tender strokes to his hardness.

His breath speeds, coming out in gasps and trembling. Mmm, I have the same effect he has on me whenever he touches me. That's good to know. Hell, it's fucking awesome.

"I can't take it anymore," he cries out, grabbing my hands and pinning them down over my head, press hard to the pillow, his lips travel over my neck, down my chest, and down more. My breath caught, I wait to feel where his tongue is leading to. A second later, his teeth rips my underwear into shreds before he lifts my legs so they are bent and spreads them as far as they go. I can feel his cool breath lingering right before my most private part on my body. My knees begin to shake, anticipating for what he was going to do. Never has anyone stared so intently at me like that, so lovingly as I watch him memorize every part on my body, commenting them to heart.

"Your so beautiful," he whisperers, his voice full of emotion before he takes me in his mouth. I let out a startle gasp, what is he doing?! His tongue comes out, moving in a up and down motion so at first, then becoming faster and faster. I bit my lip, trying to not let out what I want to, my knees buckling. My heart-is it suppose to be speeding so fast? My veins, my very skin felt on fire. The room began to heat up, feeling as if it is a 120 degrees. "Moan for my, Sapphire," he coaxes me. His tongue goes deeper into me, his finger not far behind it. Unclenched my teeth, I let out a loud moan as he thrushes in and out quickly while his tongue repeated the same up and down. Something was building deep inside of me as I couldn't stand anymore of this-it was too good to feel, so powerful and amazing it blew my mind. "No, not yet," he argued aloud, coming back up to my lips. "Chloe," he moans my name, not directly to me as if he had something to say. Mmm, the way he says my name is so pleasing to hear. Our lips met each other's again, only wanting more, demanding it as I forced my lips fastly on his. I feel him begin to enter me, slowly and careful not to hurt me. I fight back a frown, trying to ease the pain. How could I ever get use to his size? It is just too large and full.

"Want me to stop?" he asks, kissing my forehead, my cheek, then rounding his way back to my lips.

"No, don't ever stop," I moan as he went deeper in, my nails digging into his back, my own back arched up. His only response is a grin pressed on my mouth. I run my hands down over his back to his butt-and one hell of a ass at that!-and push on it, trying to make him come deeper, deeper into me. I just couldn't get any closer than we already are and it's driving me insane.

His hips move as he thrushes long, deep strides in and out, our eyes meet and hold the others there a second before his lips goes back to my arched neck and kisses it, all the while he goes on entering and going out. Our pace comes faster, my hips moving in time to him. I moan again, barely hearing the head board banging against the wall, as he moans.

"I love you, Chloe," he manages to gasp, sounding breathless and out of control, his hot eyes burning on mine.

"You better," I retort, knowing damn well I love him and not wanting to ever admit it. His eyes soften as he hears that thought. We continue making hot, fast, then slow, then fast again, love for hours, never tiring nor becoming bored. There is so many places to explore on him, and it's so amazing. There wasn't a spot on him that I left untouched or unkissed, as he did me. Finally, he lets out a loud moan before I feel him release deep in me.

"Your going to be the death of me," his stammers, his body collapsed on mine, his arms giving way. Our bodies were now sweaty as we lay there, trying to catch our breath. I contently smile at that, my heart and breaths slowing down.

"Can't-kill-a-immortal," I say in between deep breathing. How embarrassing it is when your the only one with a working heart and it pounds at a impossible speed. His hands trail over my back, lightly touching it and giving me goose bumps on my arms and neck.

"Mm, true." He kisses me on my forehead and closing his eyes, smiling, and wrapping his arms around me. I sigh, not really wanting to talk either as I was suddenly worn out. My last thought before I fell asleep was how safe and loved I feel in his arms, like never before.

"Sleepy head, wake up," someone calls, singing sweetly. I smile, knowing who exactly it is. I could never forget his velvet voice. The world's best singer would even be jealous of the flawless, sexy voice he has.

"Nope," I smile again, the P sounding popping loudly. I want to stay here forever and not be fully awake and know the betrayal I-I sharply sit up, grasping the cover to my chest. Blindly, I look around the room. This isn't my room, but Luce's.

"What's wrong?" he ask, alarmed at my expression. Oh. My. God. What the hell have I done? Drake's father, I grimace, I slept with my boyfriend's father. Twice. And what is worse is it was the best damn thing I have ever done in my life. I thought making love to him the first time was good, it wasn't nothing compared to last night's.

"Drake," I choke, standing to my feet, bringing the cover around me so he couldn't see me naked. Why not? He's already seen you, I thought bitterly to myself, overwhelmed with guilt. Can't be too much guilt, you knew what you were doing last night, but did you care? NO! I argue with myself, trying to ignore Luce.

"Don't worry about him. Chloe, I love you-love makes this alright. You can't possibly love him, can you? You were so alive last night, so beautiful, so passionate. Everything will be fine," he said in the most annoying positive tone.

Defiantly, I place my hands on my hips, spinning around to face him. "Fine? Fine? How can everything be fine! I should not of had sex with you, never. Oh, God, I cheated on my boyfriend and so soon after just entering it!" I groan, picking up my dress and quickly putting it on. My underwear was beyond repair, I grimly thought. Dang. And I really liked those.

He came to me so quickly I barely saw his body move, his hands grabbed my shoulders. "Chloe, Sapphire, it's alright. I'm sure he won't understand, but that's even better for us. Now we can date-"

"No! I don't want to break up with him," I stubbornly state, folding my arms over my chest. He'll dump me, for sure, but that doesn't mean I want to! And I sure as hell don't want him to break up with me. Great, I'm a hoe now. I had sex with another guy and want my boyfriend-the one I'm dating and only for a few days now-to stay with me. How could my life get more complicated? But sadly, I've been wrong.

"He's not going to stay with you. Maybe he will," he hiss, clearly jealous now. "Knowing my son, he'll stay with the slut."

I slap him, watching as his face sling to the other side. His eyes burn into mine, piss at me, before he spit the blood on the ground. "I am not a slut! You seduced me, you asshole! Just like the first time, or else-I wouldn't've slept with you," I retort, saying anything to make him hurt. "You don't love me, I was just an amusement to you! Hmm, I wonder what it would be like to fuck the freak," I poorly imitate his voice. He laughs, throwing his head back. Had I missed something? I frown, pulling my brows together. "Chloe, your not a freak, baby. Why would I ever use you, other than the pleasure and the feelings I get from it, there's no reason for me to. I love you, dammit," he growls, kissing me on the lips. I stood there motionless, not responding to him at all as his lips demanded mine open, his breath already coming out ragged. He pulls back, disappointment written on his sexy face. "I don't say so those words lightly, and I haven't since you were last alive. Please, believe me, my love," his hand reaches out to caress my cheek, trailing over my lips and eyes causing me to shut them. I had to admit his touch feels awesome, sending electric shots throughout my body, I want him again.

His lips land on mine, softly and slowly kissing me, but this time it wasn't demanding or lust. It reminds me of him asking a question and filled with love and tenderness. It nearly broke my hear how sad his kiss was, so I eagerly kiss him back, matching his temperament.

"Lakota!" someone calls far away, the voice echoing off the hallway walls. On impulse, I back away, feeling terrified as I recognize that soft, velvet-like voice, so much like his father's. It is Drake. "Chloe?" he calls out again, sounding alittle closer, but still far away. I run out of Luce's bedroom, jogging down the hall and turned until I found myself in his arms. Reaching up, I kiss him guiltily on the lips. Hell, it might be the last time I ever get to touch him. I can't lose him, I snarl in the back of my mind. I don't want to lose him, not now or probably ever.

"Are you okay? Did he try again? If he did," Drake begins to hiss, looking behind me. "Get away. We're leaving."

My heart drops to my stomach. Crap. Crap, he knows! How did he find out? Odin, maybe he told him! That little-my thoughts are interrupted by Luce's laughter.

"You cannot possibly think it was my fault the portals didn't work last night, can you? You know I don't have enough strength or power to do it," Luce tone was dead serious.

Could he have closed them? I mean, he has to be powerful, considering he is the Devil and extremely old. "Ugh, thanks Chloe, for that," he adds, reading my mind. The blood rushes to my face. So he does know how to read minds? Wonderful.

"I know nothing of the kind. No-one knows how strong you are, you never say!" Drake begins to lean down like a lion, hissing at him.

"Drake!" I snap at him, forcing him back up. A little too much for he almost fell back the other way, looking appalled at me. "Of course he didn't close the portals. Stop it!" I yell when he growls at his father. "Dammit, Drake, we are leaving and when we get back I want to talk to you. Alone," I add, grabbing onto his collar. This time I didn't close my eyes as we transport nor did I acknowledge the creepy voices. I am pissed, at myself, Drake, and Luce. Why did he have to act like a child towards his father? He was afraid of yet he never backed down from him. For that, I had to admire him.

"What do you want?" Drake snap, laying down on my bed. "Make it quick, you have to train with Odin after this. He demanded it once he found out-"

"Would you drop the smart ass tone? Damn, Drake, you are more aggravating than a child of two!"

He flys back onto his feet. "No I'm not! Remember, I'm six!" he retorts.

I close my eyes, trying to calm myself. What the hell is wrong with me? Normally, I can control my temper. I hardly ever yell, or shout, or anything like that. "Drake, I cheated on you," I blurt out, opening my eyes, but not looking at him.

Moments pass in silence. Say something, I beg in my head. Say something before I have to look at you. Too late; I looked and wish I didn't. His face was red, his fist tightly bawled together his sides. This isn't going to go well. "Well..." I left unfinished, hoping he'd finally speak.

"With my Father, eh?" he sneers, not looking at me. He laughs cruelly. "Should've known better than to leave you alone with him. I saw the way he kept staring at you, like you were his and not mine. Your a goddamn slut!" he snaps, finally turning to glare at me. He looks disgusted, torn in between many things. Anger, sadness, hurt, lust, love, and so much more emotions plays out on his face. "You go and fuck my father, the damned Devil? How stupid could you be?! Did you forget you are my girlfriend or did you not care as long as he filled in your legs?" he harshly asks.

"Don't you dare say such things to me. How many times have you fucked other guy's girlfriends and left them after getting what you wanted!" He places the empty space in my room and stops, to register my words.

"I'm not afraid to hurt your feeling's, Chole. I will say what I think is the truth. You know what? Yes, I like you alot and I think I could learn to fall in love with you. But I am not going to sit around and be played like a damn fool! If you can't be with just me, then it will be over. Hell, I'm thinking about breaking up with you now!" he adds, running his fingers through his hair.

I smirk at him, placing my hands on my hips. "But you won't," I saucily tell him, knowing for a fact he wouldn't let me go. "You want me, the bad with the good. Your evil, I sense that, and I hear the whispering going on around the school and not how you used to be a player, but far more dangerous, bad things. Do I care? A little," I shrug. "Not much. I want to work this out like you do. Let's just move on from this and forget about it." My hand rest on his cheek, almost like my touch causes the anger in him to disappear.

He sighs heavily. "You're hurting me, Chloe. I like you a lot and you do this to me?" He sighs again, smiling weakly at me. It was going to take time, but I knew eventually he would forgive me completely. "Fine. I forgive you, but if you ever . . ." he warns, kissing me on the forehead, his brows wrinkling. I tilt my head up to kiss him but he pulls away. My eyes water as I am moved my rejection.

"I can't, just yet," he whispers, his head hung low. How bad exactly have I hurt him? His pride looks destroyed! "'Sides, you smell like-like, well, him," he stutters, his shoulders tensing up again. "You should go."

I nod, stopping at the door before turning to him. "Drake, I'm glad you forgiven me, even though I know it will take a long time to forget. I'm willing to wait, as I hope you are too. I don't ever want to lose you. I love how dangerous and bad ass you seem to be, and yet when you are with me your sweet, charming, and teasing. Don't ever change, please. See you later," I call out, closing my apartment's door.

"Pay attention!" Odin yells, knocking me to my butt. I let out a low hiss, pissed. This was the 8th time he made me fall in less than a hour. A record for me.

"I'm trying!" I retort, gathering to my feet. He closes the distance between us in less than two long strides.

"Then try harder," he sneers, sounding like a God again. "Maybe I was wrong, it's too soon for you to be working on these kinds of techniques. Here, work with a broom instead of a sword. I wouldn't want to hurt you," his lips twist into a smirk.

"What the fuck is your problem, my lord?" I snarl the last part. How I hate having to call him that! It isn't right and it sounds so freaking old age.

His eyes grow small, stepping away from me. "Watch your tone when you speak to me," he says lowly. "How was you're night with Lucifer," he smiles wickedly. Damn him.

"You listened in to my thoughts," I state, too angry for words. My blood begins to boil over, my fist shaking.

"Not that I wanted to. But hey, at least you enjoyed screwing him." His head flies to the other side, taking in the impact of my hands to his face. Shocked, I look down at my already growing red knuckles.

"Fuck. You. Go to Hell!"

He laughs, throwing his head back before he turns back to me, looking evil and every ounce a God and Vampire. "Too late, I've already been there. In my point of view it's better than Heaven. You were there, don't you remember yet?"

My body shakes for some odd reason, finding truth in his words but not wanting to. "No," I weakly reply, lying.

He laughs evilly again, his beautiful scaring me now. He looks terrifying and filled with beauty, looking like a demon with his glaring eyes and warped mouth. "Yes, yes you do. You'll start to have flash backs when you get older. If you live," he adds, then turns. From his reaction I could tell he wasn't suppose to tell me that.

"What does that mean? If I live?" He is silent, regretting his words. "Odin?" I place my hand on his shoulder, ignoring the electricity traveling throughout my body.

He shivers, feeling it too. "Go," he replies in a dead, flat tone.

"But-but I don't understand," I stammer, not wanting to leave so early. I just got here a hour ago and still have a few more left to train with him.

"You don't need to right now. Go to the gym room," he adds in a rather odd tone, sounding like someone I couldn't put pin point but remember.

"Why?"

"Because I think you will find yourself-amused. Just go, please?" he pleads. "I need to be alone for a moment. And your blood is smelling really good, like spring time after it just rains and vanilla and roses and something else I can't explain-just go!" he yells out the last part, his body trembling badly.

I ran as fast as I could, scared of the way he was acting, not really paying attention to where I was going until I was standing outside of the gym's doors. Might as well as go in, I casually tell myself, hearing the cheers and clapping and whistling coming from inside. Our gym is huge, three or four times bigger than all high schools back in the Human Realm, so to say that this gym is filled with students, that's saying a lot. No one notices me as I stand by the door, leaning on the wall for support and trying to clear my head and make sense of all this. Why would students be in a gym after school hours and so excited.

"Hi, didn't know you support our cause, but thanks!" a tall brown hair girl smiles at me, handing me a flyer before going off in another direction to hand out more. The blood rushes out of my face, reading the note. No, this can't be right, my eyes scan over it again.

"Let's take back our world! Destroy the humans!" some yell out, clapping happily as a young looking man goes to the step up stage. I know better; looks are not always what they appear. I think I'm going to throw up.

His hand blindly hushes them. I know this man, but from where? "Good night, fellow young students at Nighting Gale. I'd like to introduce myself for all those that don't know me. I am Twe and this is Sigel," he points to a extremely tall man next to him. This isn't good, I'm getting a bad vibe from those two.

Sigel. Twe. Where do I know those name? Aren't they in Mythology or something like that? "Also, thank you all for coming and making all this possible. I am relieved to know that people care about our existence and respect. For too many years the Humans have made fun of us, dressing up as us in mockery on 'Halloween', believing we are only a myth without any facts. But that will soon change! We will get what is rightfully ours and they will get what they deserve!"

"And what is it exactly that they deserve?" my voice carries out over the room, quieting everyone and causing them to glare at me. Twe smiles easily.

"I'm glad that you ask, young child. What ever way but then to kill? As history has taught us-" he turns back to the crowd, but I refuse to stand there and listen to his bullshit.

"Actually, I am not young. Young to you, considering you're one of the oldest still alive, but older than any other student in the gym."

His smile is wiped from his face, mad I kept interrupting him so rudely. "And what is your name?" he asks, not really wanting to know. I pull my shoulders back and held my head high and proudly.

"Lakota Chloe VanHore, Daughter of the Lunar Eclipse. Why would you want to kill Humans? They have done nothing wrong." I feel everyone staring at me hatefully but I don't care. They are the monsters and I know I'm right. Well, whatever respect I had at this school is soon going to be gone.

Sigel snorts loudly. "Done nothing wrong? What haven't they done is more the question! They have ruined their own planet, killed each other over jealously, insanity, and so on. They cannot be trusted and are beneath us. They are nothing more than food, without a properly working mind. They are bias to people of different color," he hisses. Ah, so this one is more easier to make mad than Twe. Good to know.

"I beg to differ. Most of the working stuff we have here in this world was created BY Humans, and so what if they kill each other? Do we not kill our own kind? Are most of the people in this room not bias to others? BULLSHIT! I've seen how Vampires loath Werewolves, how they look at them in disgust, how they laugh and talk shit behind their backs. Without Humans our kind will die, they are more than just food! Their minds work, not as well as ours, but still. We are part Immortal, that makes us stronger, smarter then them. But wiser, more accepting, kinder? No!" I yell, losing my temper. "I know first hand how caring Humans can be, and how cruel they can become. But our kinds are the same. We have good and bad people just like they do. Who are we to judge them and say that they must die?

"We are not God, and most here are not even truly Immortal-"

"Oh and you are? You are just a Vampire-"

He cut me off so I cut him off right back. "I am Vampire, Witchan and Goddess. I am 117 years old and didn't start to grow until 17 years ago. I will not stand by and watch you kill off the Humans," I growl. Now I know why I am going to start a war; I am glad that at least it's going to be for a good, clean cause unlike them.

Twe laughs, hearing my thoughts. "You couldn't handle us, foolish woman. Watch what you say, for those are heavy words enough to start a war."

I turn to him, my stare dead and filled with coldness. "So be it," my voice echo's over and over in the room, sounding like a broken record. "You want a war? You have one," I slam the door behind me, pissed to the point of knocking the shit out of the next person I see.

"You little fucking freak, how can you think you're better than us?" a girl comes out of the room, running up to me, her face showing her disgust and hate for me.

"Think? Honey, I know I am better than you," I laugh, getting in her face, daring her to even think about hitting me. She blinks, cowardly looking to her little group of whore-friends, looking scared for her life.

"You will pay for this!" one yells out after me, but I ignore them and continue walking. The cowards, they would wait for me to turn my back and almost out of earshot. I stop, debating on whether I should go back and beat that little bitches ass, then decide I should be the adult here and act mature. They will soon get what is coming to them all. Panic rose through me. How am I going to lead a war? I don't even have any people that are willing to fight with me, let alone for Humans.

"What is wrong with you?" A black hair girl tosses her cigarette, the curls in her hair seeming soft and smooth down her back. Her eyes are black, her skin white without a tan. Vampire, something in the back of my head whispers. She's the other girl from my vision, the one that was sitting with us and laughing. Only here she appears a little bitter and lonely. "Sorry, I know who you are. I had a vision about you, so yeah, I feel like I already know you," she sighs, eyeing me once over. "Actually a lot of visions, most I'd rather not have. Do I sound crazy to you?" she asks, sitting on the curb next to me.

I laugh, staring out over the hills. "Nah, I had a vision about you too. We are going to be good friends, I am sure of it."

Her lips pout out. I don't think she is used to this kind of weirdness. "You're going to be really happy and shit around me, aren't you?" she growls, upset about that. Okay. That's not odd at all.

"Yupp," I reply, the P sound really sharp, making sure she get's the point.

She groans, lilting another cigarette. "Great," she dryly states, taking a long drag before letting it out. I watch as the smoke disappears in the air after a few seconds. "So, you going to tell me what's wrong or what?"

My fingers run through my hair, acting on their own accord. How do you tell someone you just started a war, a actual war where people will die? Better be blunt and just say it.

"I just started a war and so far I'm the only one on my side. The Vampires and Witches here want to kill the Humans and I don't agree with it at all."

She nods, taking another hit and blowing it back out, acting experienced in it and like she has smoked for years now when she only looks to be 17 or 16. "Your in deep shit now. I doubt you'll be the only one when word gets out. 'Sides, I was there, back in the Gym. Something told me to be there, which I'm a little pissed at now, seeing all that bullshit back there. Good thing you spoke up before I did, I don't have the guts to stand up to those evil twins," she fakes a shudder, grinning weakly.

"I know I don't know you well, yet, but would you like to join me in it?" I awkwardly ask, feeling out of place and uneasy.

"Oh, what the hell? We're all going to die anyways," she replies flatly. I just know she is going to be the one with the dry sense of humor. Excellent, I clap dorkishly. Two to a million, now we just got to get everyone aware of this.

"C'mon," I stand to my feet. "We have alot to do."

She groans, putting out her cigarette. "Damn. I would be the one to walk in on the wrong time. Whatever. Let's go like some Mr. Roger's and a good ole attitude about having to kill people," she grimaces, picking up her purse. "It's a wonderful day in the neighborhood," she sings loudly, not caring that she was drawing attention from others, gawking like she was a rat crawling in their soup. "What the fuck are you freaks looking at?" she snaps at them. I laugh as they quickly scatter in the opposite directions. I am going to like this one. She is blunt and straight to the point.

"So, where should we start?" Autumn calls from behind us, smiling. What is everybody's problem here with listening in?

"Excuse me?" I stupidly ask, causing them both to roll their eyes. Drake snarls, giving Dylan a nasty look before backing away. Dylan ignores it and smiles at me brightly.

"What do you except, Chloe? That we are just going to sit back and let you fight alone? Hell. No. We are you're friends, we are here for you. Anyways, I think that all of us agree with your speech back there," Dylan calmly tells me, taking Autumn's hand into his. Drake hisses, staying silent.

"I can't let you guys do that, risk your lives for something non of any of you believe in. Autumn, you're so small and fragile," I fantically tell her. I couldn't allow her to fight in it. What if she got hurt or died?

"Chlo', I'll be fine. I can fight much better than you think. 'Sides, you have no say in it. I am joining your side and that's it," Autumn stubbornly claims, making me frown at her. Fine. She can do what she wants.

"Drake?" I nervously ask, not wanting him to join us but to know that he supports our cause.

He glares at me then spits before saying, "Sorry. I don't think they should live." I figured that. He is racist against werewolves, why wouldn't he be to Humans too? "Actually, I think I'm going to sign up for Sigel and Twe's side."

"What?" I sneer, pissed.

"You fucking idiot," Dylan takes a step towards him. Drake just smirks at him, crossing his arms across his chest.

"Any other day I'd be happy to fight you. Right now I am talking to Lakota, so go bark and scratch your eyes with your feet some where else," he hisses at Dylan, then turns to me. "My choice has nothing to do with what happened yesterday. I'd rather go with Twe, he has his head on straight and is thinking clearly. Do you honestly think anyone is going to join you guys? There may be some, but nothing compared to the numbers the other side is going to have."

I felt myself grow cold inside. Let him be that way. "Fine, leave then. I have nothing else to say to you. We shouldn't speak to a enemy," I hiss at him, dismissing him with a waver of my hand. "We should put up flyers or something. Autumn-"

"I'm on it! I have the perfect thing in mind," she claps her hands together, looking excited already. "Come on, Dill Pickle, you have to help me!" she pulls Dylan off in the other direction. He looks back at me helplessly. I am so going to have to ask about them later! I have to know if they are dating or not, despite the law.

"I gotta go," the dark haired lady next to me suddenly says. "By the by, my name is October Reed. See you later Chloe," she calls behind her shoulders, smiling weakly before disappearing. Great. I'm alone now. I guess I should go back to my room or something.

On the way back I saw students giving me hateful glares, whispering to the ones next to them. Word gets around quick, I thought to myself. "Freak!" one calls. But I only smile back, nodding. Yupp, I'm the freak-the freak that wants life to be over death. I'm the horrible one hear, not the murder's.

"Thank you for the lovely compliment," I casually retort, holding my head high as I walked past them.

Chapter Four: It's All Just Too Much

Odin was upset when he found out what I had done, even though his eyes twinkled with pride, muttering something too low and fast under his breath for me to make any sense of it. When he saw that this is one thing I'm not going to drop, his shoulders sloop and he sighs heavily in defeat. "I will tell the Concile to come for a meeting. You cannot declare war without the approval of the Gods, you know. I'd like you to know that if this carries out and you have to fight, your training will be doubled as well as your martial arts class," he points out, as if that would back me down.

I smile casually at him, confident there was no way in Hell I was going to. "I know," I sung happily, rasing my sword. "Ready?"

He simply shakes his head, hands on his hips. "No, not today. Go get your friends, the meeting will start as soon as you get there. They need to be there too since they are backing you up on it. Oh, and it will be in the Golden Room." I shrug, a little more than just excited. I was going to actually go in that room, the room no student has ever been or even had a glimpse of! I am sure it is going to be marvelous, from all the rumors I have heard.

"Okay!" Finding them wasn't hard at all. They were waiting right outside for me, sitting under this huge willow tree. A Human would not of noticed them under the hanging branches and leaves, but my eye sight is slightly better so I spot them quickly. Until now that is; when I am fully turned my eye sight, hearing, movements and all that will be much better and faster not to mention the Goddess blood I have in me will be 'activated' too. "Hey, guys, we have to go to a meeting in the Golden Room," I say, hearing them take in sharp deep breaths. "The Concile has to approve of all this before it really is declared. Though it's all kind of confusing," I scratch my head, grinning. Of course, Dylan knows why.

"Well, the Concile is consisted of only the highest Gods-you know, the most powerful and oldest. They claim war unless your of Immortal blood, I know you are Chloe, but its not been at it's full potential just yet, so the rights are given to them for now. Before you even speak of it, cause I can see the unnecessary worry on your face, we are all in this together, no matter what happens," he grins at me, standing to his feet as the others did. "All for one, and one for all!" Autumn dorkishly sings out, still in her school's uniform. October groans at that, rolling her eyes.

"Great. I'm surrounded by nerds, and not just that but really odd nerds," she flatly says, putting her cigarette out. I was going to say that she really needs to quit or slow down on the nicotine when Autumn hypery talks, jumping up and down on her heels.

"Yeah, but we're the coolest nerds you'll ever meet!" she giggles, covering her mouth with her hand in a old fashion movement. Her chestnut golden hair looks even more pretty in the direct sunlight, giving it a weird tone, but stunning. I wish I had her hair color.

"Ugh," Octie groans again, shaking her head at Autumn but has a warm smile on her face. "You're not suppose to agree with me, dork."

"You guys, come on. Dork One and Nerd Two is not important right now," I say, frowning at them. "We have to go." They follow me to the room. Correction: we follow Dylan to the Golden Room. He's the only one that knows exactly where it is. For a Werewolf, I think it's kind of strange that he knows so much about Vampires, Witches, Witchans, and all that. He must really study alot. Another thing that strikes me as odd-for his looks and body build he looks like he should be playing professional football not in his room or library studying and doing homework. I guess that is just what floats his boat.

"Oh! Hey, Dill Pickle," some short brown hair girl smiles slowly at him, checking him out. "I haven't seen you in a while." She licks her lips, okay that is just rude to do with his friends standing by him and she doesn't even know for sure if one of the girls is his girlfriend. I instantly dislike this girl and from the way Autumn is glaring at her, I know she doesn't like her either.

"Hello, Jade. How're you?" Dylan ask, ignoring her batting eyelashes. She-wolf, my guts whispers at me. She smells like dandy lions and wildflowers on a warm, spring day. Its hard to believe that this tiny girl is a Werewolf. Jade looks over us quickly, barely interested in any of us.

"Vampire and Witches, and with the odd scent of Immortal blood? Dillie, whats with the new crowd? Am I too good for you so that you can't hang with your own kind? You know they will just hurt you." Her words seems innocent enough, but they are implying that he shouldn't trust nor hang out with us.

I hiss, pulling my lips back over my teeth, barring them out in the open. Her face crumbles as her body begins to shake a little. She is scared of me. How awesome, I flatly think.

"What the Hell is your damned problem?" I snarl, taking a step towards her. She minics my move by stepping back, looking terrified.

"Ooo, she said two cuss words in one sentence," I hear Autumn mutter to someone. She throws her hands up defensively, pleading with Dylan. Fuck that, she's mine-

"Lakota, calm down. She's just worried about me. History has proven many times over that friendship and unity with Vampires never work out and eventually kill each other. But it's different this time," Dylan turns back to Jade, explaining. I soften, pulling my back straight again. "There's no tension here, Jade, they will not harm me and I will no sooner hurt them."

She snorts, flipping her hair back, shooting him a look only he understood. "Whatever. I'm out of here. Just remember that," she adds, looking even more worried than before, and turning on her heels.

Autumn lets out a relieved breath she was holding, smoothing her hair down. "Uhm, can we go now?" she asks. We once again head for the room, only with no interruptions this time. Autumn leaves his side and walks by me, seeming to be upset about something.

"We are here," Dylan announces, opening a regular door. Only what inside was anything but normal. I can understand why they call this the Golden Room. Everything is trimmed and cut in a sparkling gold and white. It's impossible to even begin to describe or think about, I am not even going to try. Later, they would all agree with me how pretty it was and impossible to imagine.

"Lakota, Autumn, Dylan, welcome. Please, take the nearest seats," Odin lightly demands, sounding like the God he is, all play and teasing gone from his voice. It was a large, round table we sat at, sitting around unknown beautiful Gods and Goddess.

"Welcome, young ones," a woman with blonde-blue hair smiles at us, a odd fog around the strands of her hair. Mist, from being so cold. She is overly pretty, like the rest and looks young, around the age of 26 or so. Her eyes are a medium dark blue with extremely long eyelashes curving out. "Odin has told us what you plan," her eyes meet mine.

I clear my throat, already nervous. "Yes, what Twe and Sigel is planning is not right; someone has to stop it and I think-no, I know, this is the only way," my voice is clipped and sounding as one of them.

A man with pitch black, long wavy hair speaks, "ay, I agree. It is not our place to interfere with those of Mortal blood or otherwise, we would've taken this into our hands," he flatly states, scaring the hell out of me though the threat was not to me. I'd hate to be on their bad side.

Of course Mortal is Vampire, Werewolf and all that. Humans are just Humans, they have no special name since they die so quickly and easily and are not worthy to Mortals and

Immortals.

"You are a odd creature," another speaks, with ice icicles for hair, leaning to me. "Tell me, child, what are you?" he bears his fangs. I know this man; he's the God of Ice. I've heard only bad things about him-how ruthless and judging he is.

"Goddess, Vampire, and Witchan."

I hear a few gasp while others turned to Odin for an explanation. "How in the Hell did this get passed us, Odin? You know it's not possible for her to exist!"

His face is smooth and emotionless, glancing at them all. "Clearly it is possible or else she wouldn't be here. Surely you all remember that they didn't have a child? Apparently, they did. We didn't find out until it was too late. She was different from the rest of Mortal and even Immortal children. She didn't grow till she turned a hundred years old. I would know, I took care of her until she was about 105 years old. Then, she lived with her great-great grand niece. She is the one with the compassion for the Mortals," he adds, refusing to meet my eyes. I don't like him like this, all closed off and indifferent. This is an Odin I've never seen before. Reading the minds of my friends, I learned soon enough that this was how he normally acted.

All the faces turned to me, some appeared angry while others look amuse. "So, you have the gift then? I can hear your thoughts . . .though unusual, you really do care about the mudanes. How eventful," a rather plain but oddly pretty woman flatly speaks. "I agree," she adds, turning back to the others.

"No! Can't you all see how absurd this all is? We shouldn't let a student do this. Especially not an inexperience one!" Odin yells, making me shrink back in my seat. God voice, my mind fearfully mumbles. Had I missed something? What did the woman agree to that made Odin so mad?

"I agree, too. With Ashmir's vote."

"Agreed," some others voice. This only made Odin more pissed. How could they not be afraid of the powerful God? I wouldn't even know how to react if he ever directed his fury on me that way.

"If anyone here besides me objects speak now," he growls, leaning over the table to question them with his eyes. No one spoke a word for a few minutes, only glared back at him in that same emotionless way. 'The Pure Bloods way,' Dylan's mind told me. 'Its how all Gods and Goddess are.'

"I see," he speaks after no one still speaks up. He then throws a yellow file case onto the table, his head bowed in defeat. "Lakota, you are free to carry on with your plans."

"Odin, we expect you to at least continue on training the young child," one of the Immortals say. This time I didn't even bother to see who.

?

Chapter Five: Getting Ready

Barely two weeks had passed and we were training for the war to an point of exhaustion. Dylan seemed more excited than ever as we came closer to the day. I haven't seen or heard of Drake. I was more disappointed by his choices than I was of the others at our school. I was avoided before but it was nothing compared to now. Many people gave me disgusted looks and avoided me as if I had the plague. I found out from my friends that they had the same reaction, all expect for Dylan. His people were thrilled to be fighting against a huge group of Vampryes. None of the Vampryes from our school joined us and only a handful of Witches joined our side.

"Its bullshit. They should want to be with us, not acting as if we're the bad guys," October bitches when we are in Vampire History class.

Drake turns around in his seat, meeting my eyes before turning to her. I swear I could see alittle bit of sadness and regret in them. I don't miss him as much as I should. I mean, I miss him, of course but its hard to explain. I don't really miss him all that much.

"Because to them, you are the bad one. They see Humans as food and nothing less or more," he states flatly, causing my heart to jump like crazy.

"So, you don't agree with them? You keep saying 'them' like you're not apart of that group," I reply, ignoring October's hateful glares at me. She's never really liked him. huh. I wonder why, he's so sexy and charming. I'll have to ask her later.

His eyes turn cold, looking dead as he meets mine. "Don't be so stupid. Of course I am still apart of that group!" With that he turns back around. Fine, be that way! I shouted at him silently, deciding to read into his mind. Its the only way I can know for sure how he really feels.

'I don't know why I even let her get to me like this. I just don't understand-I let her cheat on me and forgive her but I can't forgive her choosing life over death? Honorable, what she is doing, I would never have the courage to do such a thing. I think I'm in love with her already.'

I sigh deeply, trying not to focus on that anymore. I didn't have the time to.

Later that night I decided to take a walk through the pretty forest I saw when I first got here. How my life has changed since then. Back in California, I was extremely popular and everybody wanted to know me. Here, its so different. People actually hate me for declaring war on the Vampires. I don't even know if Twe and Sigel knows yet. In a way, I hope so and in other ways I don't. My life really couldn't get more stressful. What if people here died because of me? I couldn't live with knowing I was the cause of there deaths or injuries. If I had thought Odin was working me hard before it was nothing compared to now. I actually had to spend more hours training. He's convinced I will become an assassin. I really don't mind it. I get to see him more often so I'm okay with it.

"Hey," I hear someone behind me mumbles. I know the voice without looking to see who. My body tenses up, ready for him to attack or something. "I'm not going to hurt you. I just have a message for you from Twe," Drake says, coming up next to me.

"Okay. So go on with it," I harshly reply, making his eyes grow small as he continues to glare at me.

"Fine. He knows of your plans and is offering you to back out 'before its too late.' In fact, he has requested you to see him tomorrow at-"

I cut his words off, not wanting to hear any of it. "I will not be seeing him, nor Sigel for that matter. Tell him I plan on not backing down. I will go on with it and we will win," I said, sounding much more confident than I really felt. I had to face it, the odd of us wining are not good. We just cannot get people to side with us, not much. Drake says that there are many Werewolves and Shape shifters that have already signed up for up and Autumn has convinced quite a few Witches and Witchans to fight with us, but still I'm sure it was no where as many as they probably have.

His eyes soften, his lips turning slowly into a grin. "I figured you would say something like that. Chlo', I miss you," he says, becoming serious. His hands reach out to message my shoulders just strong enough to relax me and take away all the tension I've been holding there the past few weeks. "You're to stressed out. Relax and take a breather for a few minutes. How's the dog doing?" he sneers, talking about Dylan, most likely most caring how he is.

I smack his hands off of me, getting in his face. "Listen here, Malberry. You will not talk about my friends in such a manner, you hear that? Not unless you want your ass kicked by me," I threaten, my eyes daring him to make a smart reply. His faces is painted in shock and fear. He should be scared. I know the proper moves to kill him with one finger in less than a second. He wouldn't last two minutes in a fight with me. He backs away, holding his hands in the air in defense.

"Chill, Chloe. I know you can whoop my ass anytime you wanted to. I've heard enough of how powerful you are and I'm not stupid enough to see if its true or not. I only wanted to talk to you. Chloe, I think I'm falling in love with you. I want you back."

I laugh, throwing my head back. God, he's such a horrible liar. I cannot believe he thinks I'll actually fall for that. "What, you don't care about sleeping around with many different woman anymore? Drake Malberry, you should know better than to think I would believe any of that crap," I hiss, walking back towards the school.

He follows me, then stops me by grabbing my hand and ruthfullessly pulls me to him. "Just hear me out and let me speak, please? Chloe, I'm serious. Ever since I first met you I haven't even thought about another girl, all I want is to be with you. I know I've always been a man-whore and its hard for you to believe me, but I do love you. There's just something about that drives me crazy. Sure, you annoy the Hell out of me, but I like that you put me in my place and have me wondering what your going to do next. I love how you won't give in so easily to me, how beautiful you always look, how honorable you are, how make me angry and always say what your thinking. I don't want anybody but you. I want you to be with me forever and love me back," he says touching my face tenderly.

I let out a breath I hadn't realized until now I had been holding, pulling out of his arms and ignoring the hurt look he gives me. "Drake, I don't know what to say to that. I don't love you. I'm sorry, but its true. I won't ever be with you, not after seeing the true side of you. You are willing to allow Humans to die and become nothing but food. I can't love a man like that," I sadly say, looking away from him. I would never want a man that thinks like a monster, like him.

"There's someone else then. Who is it? Its Odin, isn't it? I knew you love him. The way you look at him is so clear, its really disgusting. Even more so I think he feels the same way!" he lowly shouts, looking hurt even more. Is it true? Can he really like me that way as I do for him? Wait. Drake-up knows I have deep feelings for Odin. How is that even possible, I don't remember saying anything of the kind to him nor looking at him in the way Drake suggests.

"That's crazy. I don't like Odin and he doesn't like me. Your just imaging things," I conclude, not really lying. I don't think I like Odin, I'm in love with him. So I wasn't really lying to Drake-up. I said it in such a convincing way he had to think for a few moments before he shakes his head, stubborn as ever.

"No. I've seen it myself. He doesn't call you by your surname and here that clearly means he doesn't think of you as a student. Plus, I've seen the way he looks at you when he thinks no one is looking. His eyes soften, turning into a look of adoration and love. You may not like him but he absolutely loves you," he replies, sounding insane with jealously. I tried but miserably fail to calm my fast beating heart.

Oh, God, please, please let what he is saying be true! Words can't begin to explain what I feel towards the God\/Vampire.

"Liar. I'm done with talking about such things. Goodnight, Drake," I call, running as fast as I could away from him and questioning eyes. I couldn't stand there and lie to him like that.

Even after I undress and lay in bed, I couldn't forget what Drake had said. I'm going to ask Odin tomorrow if he really does care about me in any kind of way other than a student-teacher way. I can't help but wish he does, hope he would just pull me out of the blue and kiss me. I fell asleep thinking of him professing his love to me.

Either way, I stand corrected. My life can get more complicated, especially what happens tomorrow

Chapter Six: Parties

"Why is March 21st so important? What is the big deal about that day?" Sophia Leigh asked the class, snapping me out of my day dream. I hate having class so late sometimes. It feels as if I'm just wasting the day away, sitting in a chair while the sun is up and out. The night time is stunning but I like to spend time in the sun too. Lately, I haven't been able to do it that much.

A girl behind me answers easily, her voice sounding smooth and musical. "It's basically a holiday. Everyone over the age of 14 gets to dress up however they want and get really drunk off of Faerie liquor for a whole week starting the 21st."

I heard low chanting around me. Some of the guys even grinned and nodded to each other. I'm guessing all teenagers, no matter what race, likes to get drunk. Go figures. I never really cared for it in the Human Realm, though with all the recent crap in my life getting really trashed sounded like Heaven to me right now. Anything to relieve stress for alittle while. Even if for a night, it will be great to act my age and be care-free.

"Yess," Sophia says slowly, her face drawn in to show her disappointment in the girl's short answer. "But why do we do it?"

"Its to honor the seven High Concile?" some one puts in from the far side of the room I turn my head to see Hooven Blackshur. Word has it that the red haired, sparkling green eyes boy is very good friends with Drake. People also claim he's a big time player. From the way he winked at the girl sitting nearest to him, I didn't doubt that he could charm your pants right off. It doesn't surprise me that Drake would hang alot with him, considering he is\/was a player. I'm not sure if Drake still is or not. I heard some girls in the restroom claiming that he hasn't dated another girl since me. That he hasn't even touched another girl or woman since we broke up.

"No. C'mon, class, you all should know the answer to this. Is getting drunk the only thing you guys care to know about it?" Ugh, now she's getting mad. It really sucks when teachers get mad at the students. 'Cause then they start asking us randomly and make us look like we're stupider than shit. I especially hate being put on spot like that.

"Its a reminder to us that we should take days off and relax and enjoy our life. To be blessed and care free," the boy right in front of me speaks lowly. Regardless, she hears him and viola! Her features soften, her lips form a small smile. Its so odd how teachers seem to just light up all because someone finally knows.

"Yes! But what I am willing to guess, none of any of you know who started that law. It was Odin, our headmaster and God. Today we're going to learn about him and how he is important to our realm."

I snicker, knowing full well she wasted the whole class period from ranting on and on about old-time customs in Otherworld. There's no way we're going to be able to start that topic today. As if she read my mind, her face falls flat.

"Never mind. We'll start that tomorrow. It seems we are out of time. Good day, class. You are dismissed," she wavered her hand in the air to dismiss us. Instantly everyone was on their feet and moving quickly to the next class in the day. I was walking pass Sophia when she called me over to stay after class. My heart pounded like crazy, thinking that somehow I was in trouble though I didn't do anything wrong.

"Yes?" I ask, my voice strong and sure. If only my insides felt like that.

Her eyes narrow as she stares at me, thinking deeply. "What do you know about Sahamin?"

Only that Sahamin is the week 14 and older is allowed to drink. Oh, and we get out of school and work for that whole week. "Not much," I admit, crossing my arms.

She sighs, walking back over to her desk and grabbing a small piece of paper. Without looking up, she reaches for a pen and writes on the paper only for a short time and returns to where I'm standing. "Here," she hands the small paper to me, "I want you to go to the library and read up on the matter. Ask the librarian for help, he will know exactly what you need. I would explain it all to you, but I have classes to teach and it will take quiet awhile."

"Do you want me to go right now?"

"Of course, child. Sahamin is only a day away and you really need to be educated on the matter as soon as possible." She turns her back to me, showing the conversation is over.

I ignore the stares coming from the guys as the next class filled in and walked with my head held high, facing straight in front of me. A few even whistle as I walk past, trying desperately hard not to bump into the students walking in the door. Only when I'm out the class and down the long, grand hallway do I realize that I don't remember my way to the library. I haven't been there in since the first night I was here and this castle\/school is extremely easily to get lost in. Even my friends get confused walking around in here sometimes and they have been here for almost a year. Grasping on to what I do remember, I walk fast down and around the corridors, hoping silently to myself that I find it on my own and I don't have to stop to ask for directions. Which will royally suck, considering everyone is in class and when its over the halls will be crowded and loud again.

I open the side door at the bottom of some stairs and decide to walk outside to the main part of the school so I don't get lost inside. The walk outside is pleasant and warm. A long, wide stone sidewalk stretches out before me, breaking off and leading to 8 different ways. I stop in the middle, unsure which way to take as I glance at the buildings surrounding me. Great. Not one thing out here looks familiar to me.

"Lost, huh? Shouldn't you be in class or something?" I hear Drake ask. I look over and see him sitting up on the 3 foot tall wall a lined to the sidewalk on either sides. His shoulders are pressed to the wall while he is grinning at me like he just won a million bucks.

"Shouldn't you be in class? I'm going to the library. Or at least, I'm trying to. I forget the way."

He laughs loudly, throwing his head back dramatically before leaping off the way and stuffing his hands in his pockets. "Come on, little girl. I'll show you the way." How he constantly pops out of no where, I will never know. Thank God I did ran into him this time. I would be walking around in confusion for a good time.

"You never answered me. Why aren't you in class?" I demand, secretly knowing the response but not wanting to believe the worst of him.

"I don't feel like going to class today. I'd rather be outside somewhere. Pretty soon I won't be able to enjoy the sun so I'm trying to get as much as I can of it before summer comes and I have to go into the phase that will transform me to a Vampyre. Your lucky--Odin will have to bite you so you can become one. I hear that is a much more pleasant way to change into a Vampyre rather than doing it on ones own," he adds bitterly.

"Really?" I ask, paying half of my attention on him, the other half on mentally remembering the way to the library. I'm keeping my fingers crossed so I won't forget.

"Yeah. You have no idea just how lucky you are."

I shrug, not really caring about it. I wasn't exactly thrilled about the whole dying and undying part, only to come back thirsty for blood and craving sex. Thing is, the first two days your sexual needs are at their highest and hunger is a hourly thing. Nope, I'm not rushing the day I get turned. Though hearing that Odin will do it eased my worries. I read that usually whoever turns you, you and the bitter have a bond that lasts forever. It can be sexual, friendship, or a foe relationship. Personally, I'd like any but waking up to find I want to kill Odin, and him the same for me.

"How much longer to we get there?" I try keeping the complaint from my voice and miserably fail. It wouldn't be so bad if school regulation stated all girls have to wear high heels during school hours. And boy are the high heels they give you are high up! High enough to give the person wearing them a extra 5 inches to your height. Even still, Drake had a few inches on me, like majority of the men here. Very few are short in this realm, which is more than okay with me. I like a man that is tall and strong, a man that can lift and carry me.

"You should know that it's going to be a while before we reach the place, as large as this place is."

"And yet, you seem to know it better than most students here."

It was his turn to shrug, almost as if he was disinterested. "Yeah, as I should. I spend more time walking the halls than I do in the rooms in class. It comes in handy, especially when a beautiful woman gets lost and needs my help," he grins suddenly, looking straight ahead.

"Oh, whatever," I mumble, feeling shy. I felt my stomach get butterflies as I pushed the feeling away. Stop it, Lakota. You shouldn't like him anymore. I ignore the warm feeling I get when our shoulders accidentally brush against each others and practically jump in my skin.

For the rest of the way we remain silent, for once. I liked it alot that we could be around the other quiet and not have the awkward tension that most young people have. Neither one of us felt the need to break the silence and disturb the peacefulness that we both felt. It was actually comforting to be this way with him. I'm glad that whatever we have together, it is more than heavy kissing and touching.

"Well, here we are," he announces as I slowly recognize the thick double doors.

"Yeah. Thank you for walking me," I add, hinting that I wanted to be left alone now. I want some peace to myself and to be full focused on the topic and not him. He nods once and turns on his feet, walking off without saying another word to me. I sigh after him, watching until he disappears around the corner, positive that he knew I was looking after him from the way his shoulder stayed rigid.

"Yes, Chloe?" the librarian instantly asks when he looks up and sees me standing before him. I must of showed my shock well for he added, "I know everyone here by heart. Its common for me to know."

"Oh," I same lamely. "Sohpia Lee sent me here for a book, I'm guessing, on Sahamin. She said you would know where to find it."

He nods, gathering to his feet in one shift, livid movement. Are all Vampires smooth and graceful on their feet or what? "Yes, very well. Follow me, I know exactly what you need."

We walk past dozen of bookshelves, once again surprising me with their massive size and how largely stocked the school is. It wouldn't be a shocker if they have every book in every realm ever written in this library. That's how equipped they are seriously. Finally, we turn into one of the grand isles and stop at the far left side of it. Without even looking too hard, he finds the book and pulls it out, blowing the dust from the cover before handing it to me.

"Sorry, I haven't been able to clean most of the books lately. All my help quit on me unexpectedly," he says dryly, pointing at a lounging area. "You can read it there. If you need anything else you are more than welcome to come get me again."

Though from his tone, I thought against it. He didn't seem too happy about helping me just now and most likely wouldn't like me asking a bunch of questions.

"I'll be fine," I assured him, walking with the book in hand to the closest chair. The faster I get this over with, the better.

"Uhm, excuse me?" I call to him, he smiles and comes back to me in a rush.

"Yes?"

"It cannot be right. I'm sorry but there's got to be a mistake," I told him, pushing the book back into his hands. He shakes his head with a ever-so-slightly smirk planted on his lips. "No one goes to a party naked. Its not normal!" I add when he remains silent.

"Chloe, what exactly went on in that Mudane world? It is perfectly normal for people to show up partially naked or fully undressed. Its custom to show our respects to the Gods and Goddesses old ways. You will find that some countries here even ban clothes. From the way you are talking, people will think its not normal for you to wish against it. Some will suggest you are not right in the head, if you catch my drift," the librarian man says coolly, his bottom lip twitching.

I feel blood draining from my face as anger rises in me. "Not right in the head? No, I guess you could say that. After all, only an insane woman would declare war on her own people at such a young age, go to school at dusk, sleep with the devil, break up with her boyfriend, and worry about being naked in front of the entire school! Did I leave anything else out?" I hiss, leaning in forward to him. He mimics my move by taking a step back and placing the book in between us as if it were a shield. He better be scared of me! The way I feel right now I could fight a whole bar filled with sober people.

"Well, I have heard you are friends with a dog. There. You have everything covered now," he retorts. Bad mistake. Without thinking about it, without even blinking, my hand turns into a fist and punches him dead straight on the nose. Only I didn't stop. Nor did I try to.

His body flew backwards. Not risking a second, I jump on him and start slamming my fist into his face. I had only did it once more when someone blindly pulls me back, restraining me. My anger didn't cool, only it made it worse. I turned, using the moves Odin taught me, and attacked the person. 'STOP!' a strange voice yells in my head. I almost stop, recognizing the voice it belongs to instantly but impulsively decide against it and wham the guy again and again. I growl loudly, ignoring the sharp pain I felt inside of my head, not even that can stop the rage I feel against everyone and everything. I want to hurt people, rip their heads from their limbs, smell their blood as it slowly sheds from the body. I want to kill.

"NO!" I hear from far away. Odin. It's Odin. My movements come to a halt, I turn to the direction he is standing. "No, Chloe, don't. You must stop before you seriously hurt-" he pauses and looks at the man, "before you hurt him more. Come back, Chloe, there is no reason to act as a monster-"

"I am not a monster!" my voice thunders, echoing from the walls, sounding every bit as powerful as the beautiful man before me. His words fueled my anger, I could feel it lingering there, ready to consume me again.

"No, your not a monster, your right about that. Your just-you have had to much stress going on in your life. I should have saw this coming. Forgive me, I have not been so observative lately with your needs. It won't happen again, I assure you."

I bust out laughing, hard. "You-are-asking-for-my-forgiveness," I manage to gasp out, only to laugh again. Man, he sure is a odd God! Wait. Shouldn't he be yelling at me for fighting . . .in school, with a teacher?! Very typically of him, he answers my thoughts before I can say them aloud.

"Like I said, you are not to blame, Chloe. It was all my fault. You have had too much to deal with for someone of your age. Even someone much older would have great difficultly being able to hold everything so long as you have been doing. I am proud of you, really. Not only do you show you have a excellent, strong mind but also you show you have learned from my teachings," he nods to the men laying on the ground next to us, looking every bit dead to the world. "Now, I must help these men. I fear Jefforey and Claude may have broken bones. Claude is actually signing up for the war, you know. On your side, though I doubt I will be able to convince him to sway that side now," he sighs, flashing to them, blending over and chanting some foreign words loudly. A bright light fills the room, growing stronger and stronger as his chanting becomes louder. Suddenly, as quickly as the light came, it was gone. The man that tried to stop me earlier is the first to stir.

"God help that woman if anything ever pisses her off," he grumbles, gathering to his feet. The librarian guy just groan, putting his hand over his jaw.

"I think she broke my fucking jaw in one punch! The devil, that woman is! All I did was try to help her and she attacks me!" he whines, not moving in his place.

"Claude, watch your mouth in front of my students. Jefforey, you need to go to the hospital. I can do nothing for the broken bones you have. Next time, do not tempt my student with such words. It is immoral to say rude, ignorant things and you know this already. Time and time again, I must remind you. I'm done with that," Odin snaps, his eyes burning hotly. "Leave my presence this instant. I'll deal with you when you are healed and properly cared for."

Grumbling, Jefforey disappears from the spot he is laying, leaving without saying another word.

"I'm sorry. I didn't truly mean to hit you. I was only angry that someone would try to stop me and I didn't know who it was-" I begin but the red head boy named Claude hold his hand up to stop my words.

"Quit. I understand perfectly. I would've been mad to, only I doubt that mad, but still. There is no need to ask for forgiveness when there is nothing to forgive," he smiles brightly at me. Men. How confusing they can be. He has every right to be mad at me for hitting him like some insane woman gone hysterical and the only thing he can say is that there is nothing to forgive? Odd, just plain odd the people here are. "I'm just happy to finally meet you! I've heard so much about you, I feel as if you are a close friend already. Now, about-"

"Claude, don't," Odin says, his mouth pressed together tightly. Huh. Whats this about now? "I don't care, just don't," he adds, no doubt answering his mind".

"Uhm, did I miss something?" I ask, wanting to know what the hell is going on. Knowing Odin, he ignores my question and walks off. "Hey!" I yell out after him. No use, he keeps walking, ignoring me rudely.

"Don't ask questions you'll be afraid to hear the answer to," Claude offers to me darkly, his eyes turning pitch black at whatever he was thinking. "Now, what were you doing here? Surely checking out a book, no?"

I switch holding my weight to my other foot, uncomfortable the way he is staring at me for some reason. "Yeah."

"Its okay to be naked," he says, shocking me.

"Excuse me? How did you know what I was reading?" I demand, folding my arms across my chest.

"Easy," he picks up the book from the floor and hands it to me. "I saw it when I came in here, laying on the floor. Its okay to be naked there, mostly everyone will be. After a few shots, you won't care either. I know the Human Realm better than most so I can understand how you would feel awkward to be naked in front of everyone around you. You think that they would stare alot and be very . . . .hormonal, correct?"

I frown at him, though what he is saying is pretty close to it but not quite. "Sort of. I just don't want to be undressed out in public. It goes against everything I was ever taught growing up. Its illegal to without a shirt or pants in public in the Human Realm, you know that already. But here, its half-ass backwards. This world is so strange, I don't think I'll ever get used to it."

Chapter Seven: It Begins

"I still can't believe I have to do this," I grouch for the millionth time today, checking myself out in the mirror. Autumn has convinced me to buy a dress from the nearest mall. It's a beautiful deep purple dress that trails out behind me and hugs in all the right places without being uncomfortable. The only problem is: it covers nothing at all for my breast. I figured I'd rather just have my boobs all out in the open rather than anything else. But that doesn't make this any easier for me. Autumn laughs, not understanding my distaste for all this. She rather enjoys all this and believes it to be 'magickal.' It's still alittle hard getting used to the misspelling of magic here, too. "Do I have to go?"

"Chlo', it will be fine. Stop being so worried! It's not like everyone is going to be staring at you at every second your there. You know the rules-all students must go, unless you have a healers note. Its going to be okay. Besides, you look amazing," she gives me a once over look, smiling her approval. Her dress is a dark green with a slight cream tint to it. She looks so pretty and tiny, I have no doubt all eyes will be on her tonight. I tell her this and she just shakes her head.

"Its true and you know it. I'm glad you decided to go with my kind of nudity, or else I would be really uncomfortable," I mumble, wishing I could somehow get out of this.

"Alright, lets go and get this over with," I sigh, looking at myself one last time in her floor length mirror. Tonight is going to be a nightmare, I already know. Not that I saw a vision, actually, I haven't for a long time now, I just know its going to be. Maybe its my nerves, either way I do not want to go threw this.

"Yes, lets go! I'm so ready to party and have fun finally! All this school work and no play is really draining me dry. Did you see Jesse today? That girl is already drinking so she will be wasted by the time she gets there. I, personally, don't care that much for drinking. Oh, its such a beautiful night! A cool breeze, yet warm enough to feel as if your in a hot spring. I love this world," she adds, grinning brightly, as she hopes from one subject to the other. No surprise there--the girl is always keyed up no matter what is going on. I love her for it; it makes everything so much more interesting to have her around.

We made our way down to the grand ball room that could easily equal the size of my entire old school. It wasn't small, far from it, but it looked like a shack compared to this palace-like school. As we neared, I could hear music blaring loudly, echoing off the walls and vibrating my hears. Great, I'm going to be deaf by the end of the night, I bitterly think to myself when we reach the double doors. Two adults were standing outside them, looking over the people entering and making sure their outfits are approaite. What the hell is the point? Everyone is already baring everything, what does it matter if a dress is alittle short or too tight? Utterly pointless.

"Go on through," a sour looking woman tells us after giving her approval to us, turning quickly to the people behind us. I gulp, trying to calm my fastly beating heart, walking through the doors. I think I'm going to have a heart attack, I nervously thought, I'm going to die tonight. I don't care if I get in trouble, I don't want to be here! Autumn senses my thoughts and grabs my hand firmly, pulling me ahead to the punch table. Without

glancing too hard, she snatches a pretty bright red bottle and hands it to me.
"What is it?" I eye it suspiciously, refusing to take it until she answers me. Her eyes roll at me, sighing heavily.
"Its a Faerie drink. It will help your nerves, believe me. Drink it and you will feel better immediately. Here, take it," she repeats when I don't. I take it finally and take three large drinks, causing it to drip out of my mouth and drop from my chin. I wipe it away instantly, feeling alittle better already. I giggle childishly, covering my mouth with my hand. Her eyes widen at me in shock.
"This is really good. And your right, I do feel better already," I say before finishing the rest off and bust out laughing again. Funny, everything seems so funny all of a sudden. The ground moves and quivers on me. "Whoa," I try to balance myself, only to laugh harder at this.
"My Goddess, I forget how your not close to this world. Chloe, that was a Faerie drink-- the strongest alcohol beverage you will ever find in all worlds! You should not have drunk it so quickly! Here, lets find you a sit until it wears off alittle. If it ever does," she adds under her breath, coaxing me to the nearest sit and orders me to sit. I refuse, looking over the crowd to see if Dylan and October was here yet. No such luck, I burp loudly, ignoring the looks young girls are giving me. Fuck them all, I'll beat their asses!
"Ooh, there's Dylan! Hey, Dylan, over here!" I wave furiously, attracting his attention. Its still not fair that the men only have to come shirtless, while we are bared. A woman walks past me, causing me to gag at her.
"Ewh, put some pants on!" I yell at her. Damn sluts, they will do anything to show off their lower area. That's disgusting how some of the girls here could bare that instead of just their boobies, which to me, is a lot better than showing holes and bushes. Dylan grins, making his way finally to us. Autumn tenses up out of the corner of my eye. I look at her with question marks before turning back to him. "Hey! How are youu doing?" I slur slightly, feeling even more drunk than just a few minutes ago. At least Autumn was right, it did help my nerves and I almost forgot about being partially nude. Almost.
"Hey," he speaks, sounding oddly out of breath, gives Autumn a quick glance before turning to me again. "My God, are you drunk already?"
I snort, flipping my hair back, for it somehow managed to go down my back instead of being in the front. Thank goodness I have long hair--it will cover most of my nudeness. Nude, what a strange word. Nude, hehe. "No, I'm no where near it!" I yell alittle too loud, growing excited. He meets Autumn's eyes, whatever he found there convinces him otherwise what I told him. "I'm thirsty."
"Here," someone speaks, thrusting a long, blue bottle at me. I look up to see October dressed in a erotic red dress, looking every bit a Vampire chick, pretty and lethal. I take it without question this time, downing it even quicker than the first one. "Damn, girl, you act as if drinking is going out of style," she laughs.
"Great, Octy, that's the last thing she needs. Alot of help you are," Autumn grumbles, folding her arms, giving her a death glare. October shrugs, indifferent to her cold tone. She's used to people being cool to her, I guess, though I will never know how. She has a bad temper herself.
"She will be fine. I know its hard for you, but can you stop being a bitch for one second?

Let everyone have their fun tonight. God knows when the next time we will be able to," Octy pipes, pulling out a cigarette from her purse and lites it. I watch Autumn's face flush in anger, but she says nothing.

"As much as I hate to admit it, I agree with October," Dylan speaks, placing his hand on Autumn's shoulder. All the anger from her washes away quickly as she meets his eyes. "We should have fun tonight. We deserve it."

"Yeaah, c'mon, Autumn, drink with us! Let us dance and party and drink to we pass out or don't remember anything the next day," I giggle, loving this feeling of care-freeness. I wish I could feel like this sober, but its impossible. Too much stress in my life. No, don't think about that, I tell myself. Enjoy yourself and forget everything else.

Autumn sighs in defeat, looking totally helpless. "Fine. Someone get me something strong to drink," she orders in a sweet, innocent tone. Dylan instantly moves on his feet, making his way through the overly crowded people gathering around the table with the drinks on it. I look around me, taking in my surroundings deeply. I had been expecting it to be very different from what is it. I had thought the ball room would be decorated in dark, sinister colors, something that would make it seem less Human. Instead it is bright, pretty colors and looks perfectly normal--if you count expensive gold mirrors, black marble floors, and red with gold furniture to lounge on. They have a live band playing, even the music isn't heavy. The band--called X. E. C.-- would play many types of music, blending it every now and then for everyone to be satisfied with it. Surprisingly, alot of people were up and dancing with drinks in their hands.

We look so excluded from everyone else, I notice, much to my disappointment. Why can't people just accept what I am as easily as my friends do? It shouldn't matter what ruins through your veins, only attitudes and personalities should matter. No matter where you go, there will always be racism, I think to myself, lost in my thoughts.

"Hello, Drake," October seductively says, snapping me out of my day dreaming. Dylan was already back, with his own drink, stepping away from him. Sure enough, Drake was standing right before me, looking down at me.

"Hello, October," he says normally, looking at me intensely. I fidget in my seat, very uncomfortable from the way he is glaring at me. "You are drunk," he says to me, making it a statement and not a question. He is only one here that doesn't have anything to drink.

"Getting there," I reply, trying hard to focus on him and not the ever moving edges around him. He looks like a handsome sheet, air drying in the wind. That makes me laugh, causing his eyebrows to rise in question. "Just thinking something, is all."

His smile comes slight, not moving his eyes from me. "I see. May I have this dance? I don't believe we have ever danced before . . ." he adds lamely, holding his hand out to me. I take it, gathering slowly to my feet.

"I don't think she should be dancing and talking to the enemy," October snaps, trying to put herself between me and him. Finally, he turns to her, looking furious.

"I am no enemy to her. If you were in her shoes, I'm sure you would be doing more than just dancing with me. I remember very clearly how fast you jumped on me the first time we were alone," he says coldly, brushing her to the side and leading me to the dance floor. I throw a glance over my shoulder to see a fuming October. "Forget about her. She's just mad I never liked her," Drake says, taking me into his arms once we get to where he wants to dance. The music is now slow, so I wrap my arms around his neck as his wrap around my waist, pulling me closer than necessary.

"I don't want her to be mad at me. You were very rude to her, Drake," I complain, focusing on his handsome features. Why did I ever let him go? I should have stayed with him and never, ever let him leave. I don't know if he was telling the truth about how he feels for me, and I don't really care, but I would like to give us another chance. Though I know it can never be. He betrayed me, joining the forces with the evil side, and for that I can never truly forgive him. I know, I know, I should be able to, considering he forgave me for doing such an unforgivable act. That's him though, I didn't force him to and I cannot force myself to forgive him, when I should. Its just not a thing that can ever be forced.

"I don't care. You have to put her type in place or they will drive you insane and run all over you. Trust me, I've dealt with her kind many of times and they are all the same-- bitchy and bitter to the core. Like I said, forget about it. I'm sure she is already over it and flirting with the next man," he adds in a smug tone, pulling me even tighter to him. I blush oddly enough and relax in his arms.

"I've missed you," I whisper, pressing my forehead to his as I look into his silver, flashing eyes. His face remains unaffected by my words as he closes his eyes and our feet glides over the floor on their own accord.

"Okay," is all he says in a indifferent tone. Okay? That's all he says to say to me, is a simple 'okay'? I was just about to comment on it when my vision blurs and a wave of sickness overwhelms me. "Uh-uh, someone had more than they can handle. Come on, I'll take you to the restroom. Chloe, come on," he repeats, trying to move me. "Am I going to have to carry you?"

"Its not from drinking! Its a vision," I gasp, my eye wide open though I could see nothing at all. Only blackness. I succumb to it, desperate to know what my vision is trying to show me. I resurface moments later, gasping and breathing hard, holding back sobs I wanted to let loose.

"What? What did you see?" Drake demands. I shake my head, my eyes filling with tears. "How dare you?! How-how can that happen to me? Its my fault, my fault. No one to blame but my own choices. Oh, God, don't let it happen!" I finally let out a harsh sob, collapsing to the ground. Drake bends down to me, once again trying to get me to go some where else.

"What is it, Chloe? Tell me what is making your heart fill with sorrow and despair! I need to know," he says, sounding every bit as distraught as I felt. Good, he should! After seeing what the future will bring, I don't even want to talk to him ever again. "Chloe-"

"Leave her alone," a powerful voice commands, standing right next to me. "She needs comfort right now, not orders. Chloe?" he speaks to me, taking his finger and placing it under my chin to lift it up to him. Tears strike my face, coming down as fast as rain drops on a summer day down pour in the south. His kind hand wipes them away eagerly, his face masked in misery. Its Odin's face, normally so calm and stone hard, is now gloomy and down right miserable.

"I don't want it to happen!" I cry in anguish, not really noticing how everyone was looking at us. "Its not fair; I'm too young, too trusting, too-"

"Shh," he soothes me, bending farther over, picks me up and holds me in his arms like a groom would carry his newly wedded wife over the threshold. "We'll take about it shortly. Just hold onto me. Do not be ashamed to cry, for you deserve to cry a million tears." He walks to the double doors that me and Autumn came though not even two hours ago. I knew this night would end in the wrong way. I didn't need a damned vision to tell me that much. Why can't I just have a normal, relaxing day without anything to screw it up? Because I was meant to go through Hell before dying, I answer to myself. I'm better off dead, I am convinced.

Odin stops dead in his tracks and glares at me angrily at me. "Don't ever let me hear such a dreadful thought come from you! You are never better off dead in a grave, rotten, never. Its always the darkest before sunrise," he chokes back something. I look up to see his face stone hard again, the cold Immortal has returned, only his eyes show his sorrow. Why should he be sad? Surely he saw my vision, that is why he came to me so quickly. But he has no reason to be upset, none whatsoever, other than the fact he is my mentor. Something told me that it was more than that, something that I will never know unless he willingly tells me. Judging from his face, I know that will never happen.

"I have no sun rise in my future! You know that," I sneer at him, wanting to lash out and hurt him with every might and ounce of being in me. I suddenly burst back out tears, sobbing even harder now, feeling guilty and so sad. "I'm sorry. I don't mean it," I manage to get out, burying my face in his chest while placing my arms about him. He sighs and puts me back down on my feet, giving enough space between us, and stares thoughtfully at me.

"There is little we can do about your . . .future situation," he finally rests on a word. Ha, good way to put it, my Lord! The future is near, not so far away.

"That's all you can say about it? Well, I don't need your help to fix it! I'm not even going to bother changing the future. What will happen will happen. Isn't that the way it's suppose to be, anyway?" I hiss, though not really asking. I know what must be done. I know what must happen naturally, even if its going to hurt worse than anything ever before, even though its going to tear me apart to do it. It must be done.

He takes a step forward to me, looking wild and crazy, and takes my shoulders into his hands forcibly. "No, no, no, I will not allow that. I won't let anything harm you or make you suffer anymore. Look at me, Chloe, realize that I am here! Do not shut yourself away and turn from me. I am your mentor, your protector and always will be," he whispers in a strong, sturdy voice, coming alittle closer. I mimic his movement by taking a step back, smacking his hands off of me. You cannot do anything about it! I scream inside my head at him, replaying the vision over in my head, lingering on certain parts. His face turns paler than what it normally is while his lips quiver once. "Why are you doing this to me?" he wails, dropping to his knees before me. "Why must you replay what I do not want to see? It pains me to see a student of mine-"

"It hurts YOU, you? How do you think I feel? Well, I feel just fucking peachy! Its not every day your own mentor says there's 'little we can do to change the future, but hey, we can.' Do you know how confusing you are? You must not be hearing yourself talk! God damn you, I wish you back to the Hell you came from!" I scream, pushing him away, sounding just like a powerful being. "Your as heartless as the mask you put on. You care only for yourself and will allow others to die because of your own beliefs. Other than in class, I never want to see or speak to you again. I don't want you training me, I don't want to see that horrible beautiful Immortal face of yours, I don't want to hear your voice, I don't even want to think about you," I say, sounding eerily calm and detached from myself. I felt numb, terribly numb. I no longer felt drunk and giggly and happy. Instead, my heart was filled with bitterness and betrayal. No longer will I let myself trust someone as I had trusted him. I'm sick and tired of being betrayed. I want to go home to my Human Realm. I want my normal life back. I don't even care if I have to wake up at the crack of dawn every morning for school. That's better than this miserable life.

"If that is what you wish, then it shall be. I'll have someone else take over the training for you, but you will always be my student. Once the Gods have spoken about the chosing between a mentor and a student, it is usually a life thing," he says, sounding as detached as me. He gathers back up on his feet slowly, looking drained and tired.

"Then its a good thing that won't be too long," I sneer, my words causing him to flinch. Good, he should be pained. I'm glad I finally see him for the monster he really is. "I'm retiring to my chambers. I suddenly don't feel up to partying anymore. If that is okay with you, my Lord." I cannot believe I have to keep calling him that. He shouldn't be able to be called that.

"If that is what you truly desire . . ." he lets his voice trail off, no longer looking at me. I never answer him as I walk out of his room, slamming the door shut behind me. I don't even take a step before I grasp the wall for support and begin to really bawl my eyes out.

Chapter Eight: The War

I can't see! I yell at myself in my mind, once again trying to see the future. I know that I won't ever be able able to make them come at will, but that doesn't stop me from having hope. I need to know, I whisper lowly in my head to the Gods, I need to know what the out come of tomorrow will be. Show me, give me some sort of sign. Let me know I'm heading in the right direction. I never got it though. Great. I guess we'll all just have to guess about our deaths and battles. Why can't my visions show me something useful? Instead of showing me disturbing and sometimes uninteresting things that I wouldn't need to know in the first place.

"Relax, Lakota, you will wear your mind out. You will need all the strength you can get tomorrow," Odin speaks, stepping into my tent. I grimace at him then continue my pacing, gnawing at the skin around my nails. Crap, crap. I need to see, I have to know!

"Lakota!"

I stop, placing my hands at my waist, looking every bit defiant and crazy. "What?" I snap. Leave me be. I told you I didn't want to see you . . .

"I know, I know. I figured it will be okay, considering its the last night-" he lets his voice trail off, sounding eerily sad. Humrph. Look at him, sitting on my cot as if he owns it, eyeing my things on the fold out table. There's no so thing as privacy when it comes to a Immortal, I realized that awhile ago. I catch myself being the same way every now and then. Never as often as he does it.

"Yeah, whatever. Why are you here? Make it quick and be on your way," I bitterly say, yet in a calm tone, sitting next to him. I ignore the rush I feel being so close to him. The rush I always get from him, no matter how angry he makes, I cannot deny my feelings for this creature. That doesn't mean that I can't be bitter and rude towards him, though, I think to myself, satisfied when he throws me a semi-hurt look my way. He turns to me, crossing his leg over the other comfortably.

"I wanted to wish you luck. I know you probably won't need it, for you are a fine-"

"Your right. I won't need it. My future is already set in stone, Odin. Wishing someone luck won't change that," I point out, cutting his words short.

"Would you let me speak and just be hushed for a few minutes?" his face turns red with annoyance. "I'm truly sorry for everything, Lakota. I really am. If I had it my way, things for you would have turned out differently."

"Oh, like how?" I enquire, interested on what he had to suddenly say. His smile fades slowly and he turns his head back the other way. No answer. "Get out," I demand, growing angry at him. I didn't know why but the sight of him made me want to punch something repeatedly. The sight of him made me want to bask in his beauty. I can't take this! He brings me too many confusing feelings. I don't like this--feeling as if I was riding a rollercoaster of different emotions.

"Why? How do you see me so differently than other people do?" he whispers, his glaze fixed on nothing, staring into outer space. My eyebrows wrinkle in.

"What? I don't, at least I don't think so. I try not to read people's minds, like you do, so I wouldn't know how differently I see you from others. I'm sure its nearly the same," I add, getting a little nervous.

His head shakes in disagreement. "No, you don't. You see me as humane, kind, powerful, fast, touching, light hearted. Many others see me only as beautiful and powerful, but you see everything in me. Things that I am not and never were or will be. I find your thoughts to be very comforting when I am--upset about myself."

Lovely. He thinks my thoughts are comforting, nothing like a good old reminder to let me know he is still technically my mentor, my lord, my God. "Why would you ever be upset about yourself? That's just plain stupid."

"Is it? Have you ever killed someone, Lakota? No, I can tell by the innocence of your nature you have not, even before your mind answers me. Tomorrow, you will find out the horrors, the nightmares that will come with it all later on. You will regret murdering them, even if they are purely evil, they are still alive--and thats the last thought that will linger in your mind while you are trying to sleep. There is still time for you. I can take you away from all this, just say the words and I will lead the war and I'll find you a safe place to hide until its all over. I'm begging you, don't go to battle!"

His words shocks me, causing my mouth to hang open. He would lead the war, HIM, that didn't want this started from beginning- just to protect his student? No. "I have to do this. I know in my hear its something I have to go on with. What happens to me is not important as long as we win the war. The Humans will have life and be free."

His face turns cold and angry. "Not important! Bull shit, Lakota, and you know it! I will drag you out of here if that is what it takes."

"You wouldn't dare. You know how I know that? Your too honorable to do such a thing. Besides, I should be allowed free will. This is what I choose. I cannot abandon my people. I'm not that cruel and heartless as you can be sometimes! I wouldn't ever, ever do that," I firmly say. "I think you should go."

His face turns to remorse, looking sorry now. Too late! He is just as heartless as they say, like all Gods!

"I am sorry. I don't know what has come over me. Forgive me. I will step a side and let you do what you think you must. I'm sorry," he repeats again, stepping closer to me and before I even know what is going on, his arms wrap tightly around me, pulling me up against him. I couldn't feel a heart beat, though I should. He doesn't have one, I thought sadly to myself, his heart has stopped beating for many, many years. I could feel everything from just that one hug; his regret, guilt, sadness, and happiness. There is so much I want to just blurt out. I can't. It wouldn't be right, I know that but you can't help what you feel. I'm not even sure if I want these feelings to go away. I want to hold onto him forever and never let him go. If I move my head in a inch or so our lips will be touching, I realize, shaking myself to the core. Do it! something yells inside of me. Kiss him, kiss him! No, I yell back, in anguish. He doesn't feel the same for me. Those cold yet beautiful, odd eyes show that.

He finally pulls away, the mask concealing his emotions once more. Damn him. All my thoughts return to me. I was suppose to be mad at him, he was suppose to leave. I didn't even want to see him, now all that is gone. I can't stay mad at him for too long, its physically impossible. No matter how hard I try, I forgive him for everything.

"Don't," he chokes out, sounding very strange, turning away from me. "Please don't forgive me. All this-it's my fault and what will happen tomorrow . . ." his voice trails off. I automatically take a step towards him, placing a hand on his shoulder to comfort him, trying unsuccessfully to ignore the rush of desire when my hand touches his bare shoulder.

"It is not, Odin. I knew what I was getting myself into from the beginning. When it happens, just let it happen. Promise me that, okay? Promise," I repeat when he remains silent. "Odin! You HAVE to. It isn't in my fate to-" I stop short, unable to finish the sentence, suddenly overwhelmed with many emotions. I choke back a cry, willing the tears to go back where they belong in my eyes and not down my cheeks. I don't want to . . .no, don't even think it! "Leave, please just go. I can't break down in front of you," I plead, blurting the words out without even thinking about them.

His hand reaches out to me but I step back away from it, shaking my head side to side, ready to cave in. "No, please, leave." I snap my eyes shut, trying to calm my out-of-no-where-panic-attack.

"Chloe? Odin said you needed me . . . Hey, whats wrong?" I heard alarm in Dylan's voice before I even looked at him.

I shake my head, unable to answer him. Afraid if I do, I'll bust out into tears. I can't take this. I'm too young for all this. I'm just a girl that somehow woke up one day over a hundred years old! One day 16, the next --so much older. And tomorrow . . .I already KNOW whats going to happen to me. Visions suck. They show you useless things and when it comes to the most important ones, nothing.

"Chloe, you're not listening to me. Tell me whats wrong," his voice snaps me out of my little day dream, unfortunately pulling me back to this Hell-on-Earth. Without another word, his arms wrap around my waist and gathers me closely to him. His smell is relaxing, calming my erratic heart beat almost instantly. Its a nice just got cut grass, a

warm but breezy day, the air stuck to his skin, and forest smell. Its hard to explain in my head, but my souls oddly knows the smell, like a family member would recognize another after being 50 years a part. Maybe we were best friends in another life. I'd have to ask Autumn about that; she'd know. And then it hits me hard. Really hard this time. I won't be able to ask her . . . A wail escapes my lips the second my legs threaten to give out. "Shhh, it's gonna be okay. I know it will, whatever's wrong with you. Everything will work out just fine. You'll see. So, there's no point wasting tears on something silly like teenaged-old lady emotions," he grins, trying to lighten the mood. It doesn't work.
"I'm NOT OLD!" I scream out the last part. "I don't care what anyone says, I'm not that old! I'm not! There is just no way that's possible. I don't remember anything and if I lived that long, I would have! It doesn't make any damned sense. Odin HAS to be lying about that. He has to be. There-"
"Okay, okay. Your not old, then. I was only teasing you, Chlo'. You forget--in this world your still considered a child if your under the age of 200. Well. If your a turned Vampire or a Immortal. Still, your both. So, your not old."
I take a deep breath, another, and then another before speaking. "I know. So, Autumn, huh?"
His eyes become guarded as his body tenses. "What do you mean by that?" he asks in a closed off tone, crossing his arms across his chest. I walk slowly past him to sit on my cot.
"I see the way you look at her, the way she looks at you . . ."
"It isn't anything like that," he snaps defensively. "You got a lot of nerve. You and Odin, giving each other gooey eyes and love sick pouts-"
"This is so not about me and him. 'Sides, nothing is going on in that department, unfortunately. You don't have to lie to me, Dylan. It's not like I'm going to tell everyone. You love her, don't you?" I ask in a hushed voice, almost whispering it. He snorts and sits down next to me, sighing heavily.
"That's not really a question."
"Well?"
"That's not really a question, either," he snaps back, confirming my beliefs.
"Do you or do you not love her?" I ask impatiently. "Just tell me, for God's sake. I'm not going to go around boasting about it-"
"Yes, I love her! There, does that make you happy? That I've finally admitted it? There isn't a damn thing I can do about it either. Its against the law! I'm NOT going to endanger her life. I don't give a flying shit about mine, but hers-she is too special. I know she loves me too, but I won't say it back to her. I can't," he cries in anguish.
"Just tell her, Dylan. How do you even know she feels the same way? Have you asked her or something like that?"
"No. It's just the way she acts around me, when you all are not around with us. When its just me and her in my room. She gets really close to me and leans in to me like she wants me to kiss her. One time, she spent the night over my apartment, and in her sleep she whispered she loved me when she thought me to be sleeping. I wanted so badly to tell her I wasn't sleeping and that I love her too, but I can't. Not without risking both our lives. I don't want us to end up like your parents did, Chloe. As much as it hurts to be without

her, it would hurt worse to know I would be the cause of her death. I can't put her life on the line like that. She is simply amazing, words cannot even begin to explain how I feel towards her. You know, I had this huge crush on you before I met-no, saw her. It was love at first sight. Suddenly, nothing mattered anymore but her. I knew I had to have her, no matter what it took. Until I found out she is a Witch. The feelings remain the same, but I won't pursue it."

I was silent for a moment, taking his words in, thinking about Odin and me, Autumn and him. It was love at first sight for me too. Maybe it's a non-Human thing. Maybe its the God's way of putting us through Hell in life. Maybe it's just the way the world is. Love sucks and then you fall even harder in love and in the end you realize it'll never work out for any type of reason it may be. Either he don't feel the same or it's illegal. I should start a protest and call it 'legalize love.'

It will be like that case in Barstow . . .A white woman has openly--and illegally--married a black man and now both are going to trial, but not before the man was "accidentally pushed down a mountain and appears to have strange black and blue markings on his skin." It was and probably still is the talk of the town. Rumor has it that the woman has been told to say she was 'forced' to marry the man so she would walk away from the criminal charges unharmed. I don't understand what is the big deal about people marrying others out of their race. Love is love.

"Do you love him?" Dylan suddenly asks, pulling me out of my deep thinking and causing me to jump a little.

"Who?"

"Odin, of course. Or is there another man that you are in romance with?" he simply implies Drake, raising his eyebrows. Its my turn to sigh heavily.

"I do love Odin. I love everything about him, he's just so perfect to me. I fell deeply in love with him at first sight, hung onto every word he said and committed them all to memory. He won't have me though. I know it. I'm just a student to him, he's just a mentor to me in his mind. He hasn't ever touched me, not even in training. He did get angry when he found out I slept with Lucifer-"

"My goodness, you slept with the Devil?!"

I grimace, thinking back to it. "Yeah, Drake's father. I slept with him while we were dating."

He throws his head back and roars with laughing, laughing so hardly he shakes the bed. "I'm happy to see you enjoy all this," I hiss grimly. "I believe I have just egged on my face, admitting to all this."

"Don't be embarrassed! I'm happy to know I'm not the only one with relationship problems," he smugly replies causing me to roll my eyes.

"Yeah, sure. It's getting late . . ."

"And we have a war to fight tomorrow," he finishes, gathering himself to his feet. "Well, morrow. Have a good night's sleep and don't worry about all of it. I'm sure time will work everything out itself in due time."

"But for the time being, it's going to hurt. A lot. Morrow, Dylan. Make sure you sleep well," I add as he walks out of my tent.

Time won't work it all out. I don't have much time left . . .

"Are you ready?" someone asks me. I don't bother to look to see where the voice is coming from. It doesn't really matter.

"Yes," I say. And I'm honestly not lying; I mean it. I am ready for what is about to happen in the next hour. The horse below me snorts as if he is in disagreement with what I just said. Without thinking about it, I pet his neck reassuringly. Turning to the people and ignoring the gathering crowd across the plains, I glance over them all. Its incredible how many people my friends have managed to side with us. Without a doubt, our army is much smaller than Twe's and Sigel's, but that won't matter. All that matter is we will try, we will fight. 'Till death we stand. Together, we fall. I know I should make some kind of speech, something that will be remembered forever and later put into history books, but I can't speak. I can't lie so I'll say the truth to them.

"Today, we have gathered together for a good cause. We may lose, we may all die out there. Their army is too great compared to ours. That doesn't really matter though. People will know that someone took a stand against them, someone actually cared about life and risked their's for that belief. Let it be known we tried, no matter what happens to-day. I want to thank each and everyone of you for joining us in this possible hopeless war. 'Till death we stand," I add, turning back to the fields and charging out after them with my sword in my right hand. Behind me I hear the roars and shouts of my soldiers cheering. The only thing I can think of at this point is how stupid and pointless my speech was. I was better off saying nothing.

Twe's army runs out after us, their number of people seems to grow larger and larger as we near them. I gulp in fear, wanting to run back the other way and say forget it all. The Humans can die just let us live. I don't. I get off my horse and push him away, whispering to him to run from is. I hope he doesn't get hurt. That would be terrible.

Standing in front of my people, I get the first kill, fastly moving my blade through a man's body, cutting him into two before moving to the next nearest one. My reflects are kicking up, catching every movement in slow motion and just in time to save my own ass then swiftly moving and killing the person willing to strike me first. Ignoring the cries all around, I stab one after another moving with impossible speed. Somehow I end up with two swords and use them to my advantage, killing twice as fast and as many. Then I see Twe, stabbing a man ruthlessly. Instantly, I throw the swords in the air and snap the girls neck before me and catch the swords back into my hands just in time, heading straight to him in fierce determination. Get him, get him, I repeat endlessly in my mind, not even looking at the people I kill on my way to the bastard. He finally spots me and grins half jogging to me. I break out into a run, raising my swords, ready to strike and end his life as soon as possible. If I can kill both leaders then we win the war. Then their side will show their white flag and retreat forever.

"Lakota! DON'T!" someone vaguely familiar screams. I glance up to see Odin. Odin, my love. What is he doing here? I thought he wasn't going to-

"Goodbye, Lakota," Twe sneers and oddly enough my body jerks back on its own. Confused, I bring my sword back up and cut his head off, watching it fly over to the left and bounce a few times off the ground. Gasping, I collapse to the ground in pain.

"What the . . ." I whisper in a weak voice, my hand automatically going to my chest. Blood, blood. Was I stabbed? Funny, I don't think Twe did it, but I don't remember anyone else being that close to me but him. Why doesn't it hurt any? I think as my knees give in and my face goes straight to the ground.

"Oh my God, Lakota, Lakota," Odin cries, sounding close to me. I feel someone wrap their arms around me and bring me to their arms. Opening my eyes I see him. God. He looks more like a God more than ever, so darn beautiful and perfect. Always.

"What-are-you doing here?" I manage to say finally, trying to not wince when he picks me up and moves me. I cry out in pain when he sits back down on the ground, wrapping his arms tighter around me. Everything seems so blurry and hazy. I forget why I was suppose to be mad at him. Oh well, it must not be too important or else I'd remember.

I feel his shoulders shake. "Don't. Try to remember, Lakota. Hold on."

Hold on to what? Him? I try to move my arms and wrap them around him but they won't even move. I giggle, feeling even more light headed. This is the first time we actually touched and something tells me that it isn't a good thing. Which is really weird. Us touching should mean the best thing ever in this life. I'm getting what I always wanted.

"Chloe. Holy fuck," another voice says when I close my eyes. Is that Drake? It surely sounds like him. But he wouldn't be here. He hates that I'm fighting for Humans. "She's hurt! Odin, do something!" a voice I can't remember cries, clearly in pain.

"I can't," he replies, sounding in far more pain than the other boy's voice, his arms shaking even worse. "We knew this would happen, she said it was fine with her. She saw the vision, nothing would change her mind. I can't heal her, its too late for that."

"CHANGE HER! DO it! Please, please, saver her, Odin. I can't live without her. Don't let her die. She has to live . . ."

"I can't change her. It's against the law. Besides, it would complicate things later. You know that. I'm sorry. She has to die, it is her fate."

"No, no, no, no. If you love her, you won't let her die. Do it for yourself, for you two. You love her, I can see that. Save her, don't let her die again. Please, I'm begging you. I'll give you anything, anything if you just do this. Please."

I wanted to call out and say something, anything to wash away the pain the two voices seemed to be having right now but I couldn't open my mouth. I couldn't speak let alone make any sound. I no longer cared to. Something wet drips to my cheeks. Huh. When did it start raining? I know for a fact today wasn't going to rain . . .And that Light. My eyes are closed but this light is getting brighter and brighter. Not in the kind of way that hurts, but as in a comforting and beckoning light. I want to follow it and see if there's anything in it but my gut tells me not to, not just yet, hold on. But hold on to what, I don't know.

"She's dying," someone chokes. "Her thoughts are dimming now."

"No, no. Don't let her die. I love her as much as you love her. Save her, save US."

The voices getting farther and farther away until I can barely hear them and then, nothing at all. Just peacefulness and calmness. Nothing can touch me, nothing can hurt me anymore. Nothing at all is important nor do I care. I open my eyes one last time to lay my eyes on him.

"I love you," I whisper lowly and close my eyes again for the last time. . . .

I open my eyes and see a forest all around me. I choose to ignore it. My love, my life is standing right before me, looking in deep pain.

"You gave up on life . . ." he whispers to me, wrapping his arms around my waist. A tear escapes my eyes and trails down my face but not before long he wipes it away quickly with his plam, his hand lingering there tenderly.

"There was nothing to live for," I reply. He shakes his head once, looking me deeply in the eyes.

"You had me."

"No, I didn't," I cry, my knees giving in once more. He catches me instantly and we both fall to the ground softly. "You were always so far away. You didn't and don't care about me. I know that now."

"No, that isn't so. Look at me, Lakota. Kiss me once more," he eagerly says. I look up the same instant our lips meet, crashing and melting as if they have done this a million and one times.

"A million and two times," he answers my thoughts when we break apart. "I love you, my little love. Why can't you see it? How are you so blind to me in waking life? I love you," he repeats. "It's time to wake up. You've been sleeping too long . . ."

"No, I want to stay here with you," I stubbornly say, tightening my hold on him knowing it won't work.

"Goodbye, my love."

I gasp painfully, standing up right, with my eyes still closed. I'm afraid to open my eyes and see what world I am in. Most likely Hell, or something much worse.

"She's awake!" a voice yells. "Thank the Lord, she's awake!"

Chapter Nine: Waking Up

I groan at the overly high pitch voice. Urgh. Could you be any louder? I ask silently, finding I couldn't yet speak or talk.

"You all should leave. Now," a powerful yet soft voice commands, sounding like more music than a voice ever should be able to. I automatically listen closely to hear his sweet voice again. Odin, something in me shakes, recognizing him finally. His name is Odin Omay, my heart aches for him. I cringe back on the surface I'm laying on.

"She's even more beautiful than she was before," someone whispers, sounding in a daze, but clearly a boy's voice on the edge of becoming a man. This one I didn't know, but I felt as if I should. Like I should know my name, I should know his. I hear a few mumbles in agreement and frown slightly at this. I admit it, I'm pretty but I'm not beautiful. They say a Vampyre looks changes once they have been Bitten. I wonder what I look like now, secretly hoping the blonde hair will never return and my eyes remain the unique purple color I have grown fond of.

"Yes," Odin sighs. "Now. Leave," he hisses. "What will happen will embarrass her undoubtfully and I wish against it. Besides, I have things I wish to speak in private with her about. Why am I explaining myself? I am a teacher, your advisor, your principal! When I say leave, leave."

I hear a few crashes and a groan, but soon the room goes quiet and I can literally feel the room is empty. But one person. The person I feel even more inclined to love now.

"Odin," I manage to mumble out, my voice shaky and dry. I was beginning to feel hungry. A much different hungry from what I ever felt in my life. This was a nagging, desperate hungry. I had to eat and very soon or else I might go crazy. I felt on edge, like I was living in a world of panic attacks, ready to gnaw on my finger's skin and pull my hair out.

"Here," he says, bringing a straw up to my lips. The aroma fills my nose, getting a huge, wonderful weft of something so sweet, sour, and perfect. "Drink this, it will help you." I easily do so, eager to taste it.

Almost immediately my senses are heightened, my skin ever so that I feel as if I have extra sensitive skin, I could hear everything so much better, I could FEEL Odin better. It was like me and him were almost the same person, yet no so much. It is confusing to me. My anger starts to grow.

"Now, now. I'll explain everything in a short time. Just relax now, be as comfortable as you can be, Chloe. Open your eyes," he adds, whispering directly by my left ear, his lips brushing on them. My eyes open on their own accord, my body is suddenly his to command and not mine.

"Odin," I gasp, seeing him in a way I have never before. Everything about him was so much more beautiful, more perfect yet flawed at the same time. His blue-green eyes are darker and more intense, his face more smooth and carved like a God's, his body more hard and dangerous looking. Everything about him screamed he is a God, but something lingered on him in such a light, wholly goodness way made me believe he is something more than just Vampyre and God. What IS he? His eyes bore into mine for a few seconds before they trace over me, lingering in certain spots that made me blush with pleasure. Finally, he sees me! Actually sees me.

"The substance I gave you was blood," he blurts, sounding shaky and moved by something unknown to me, looking away out the window near my bed. Truly, I was in my own bed and apartment. "Not mine as it should have been. We will have to continue the exchange of blood until your body replaces all the Human blood left in your veins. You have a closed heart," he explains, "The Human blood will stay there until your heart pumps in only Vampire blood. Then your heart will completely stop beating and you will fully be a creature of the night. A person of Nightinggale. I-I must warn you," he stutters and fails to speak clearly.

"Yes? Go on," I urge, my own voice sounding strange and foreign to me. I like this new voice better though. Its full, powerful, sweet.

"There-there will be certain things you will feel when we exchange blood," his face rushes with blood. Ha! He is finally blushing! The Great Odin is finally embarrassed. I grin at his words, somewhat understanding.

"And what will that be? Will you feel whatever it is too?"

"Sexual desires. I don't know. I have Changed many before and never felt it, but that can change as quickly as the blood in your veins. Everyone feels things differently with other people," he assures me oddly enough. "We may not feel anything at all."

I seriously hope that won't be so. I grin slyly at him, causing his head to turn in the other direction.

"You have changed," he whispers carefully, his voice barely grazing the tips of my ears.

"Huh?" was all I could muster up. God, I'm an idiot. Finally, he turns completely back to me and stalks over, his face masked with an expressionless look. The old Odin is back. Hoor-ray, I thought to my self miserably.

"Your--appearance. It has changed tremendously. You were fine before . . .but now . . ." his voice trails off. Why do I keep hearing this? How much exactly have I changed? I jump out of my bed and run to the nearest floor length mirror, located behind my bedroom doors and take intake a sharp breath. I'm gorgeous, I think to myself in wonder and amazement. Reaching out with my fingers, I touch my reflection on the glass, lingering on my face. Odin walks up behind me with a small smile and approval shining brightly in his eyes.

"Yes, yes, you are," he whispers, just barely loud enough for me to hear. I blush, still looking at my self. The new and permanent me.

My eyes-they were purple before, but now they are a violet flower purple with a very slight tint of blue and yellow, twinkling as luminous as Odin's. My eyebrows looked thinner and a little more arched with longer, thinker, blacker eye lashes to set off my amazing new eyes. My hair was noticeably thicker with a more purple hue to it. My skin was a few shades darker than what it used to be and looked and felt so much more smoother to the touch. My neck was slimmer and more defined. My own breast were fuller and more--higher. I pull my shirt up to reveal a smaller, flatter stomach. Leaving it there in a daze, my eyes travel to my legs and even those are more muscled yet womanly and perfectly shaped to go correctly with my firmer and fuller buttocks.

"You are beautiful. You have a true hourglass. Look at how your bloosm fills out and your curves come in and out perfectly. You are a true Goddess," Odin speaks in awe, his hand coming out to run over slowly my stomach. The hairs on my arms react instantly and are standing up at his touch.

His soft, strong hand gently pushes my back so that I am pressed tightly against the curves of his body. I glance at our reflection and stop. The image captures my attention almost whole heartedly. We look so perfect together. Just so right. How could this ever be wrong when everything about it screams at me it is right? That we were meant to hold each other like this?

Odin's eyes droop with lust while his lip pouts a little, making me want to desperately kiss those full, sensual lips. His hand stops, his eyes meet mine dead on. I want you, his eyes tell me as his head slowly moves in. Inch by slow, painful inch. I wait for it, closing my eyes, my stomach still filled with butterflies from the very way he just looked at me. I can feel his breath on my lips, pausing there as if he is still deciding whether or not to actually kiss me. I lean in for encouragement-

"Chloe! Your up!" Drake practically yells at me. I clench my hands into fists and hiss at him. He laughs easily and shakes his head. "You know, that's not very attractive. Though, I suppose, you could pull it off. Come hither, my love. Let me take a gander at you," he speaks teasingly but his eyes flashes a hunger at me. I circle the room around me, looking for Odin while Drake's own eyes trail over me over and over again. He whistles. "My, my, my. You were beautiful before. I honestly didn't think one could get more attractive and womanly and so damned available," he growls the last part out.

He's no longer here. He must have heard Drake's thoughts and vanished. Damn Drake. "How is everyone? Please tell me no one died! I couldn't bare a death on our hands. Where is Autumn, October, and Dylan? Why aren't they here, too? Oh Goodness, something has happened to them. How badly are they hurt?" I demand, firing questions at him repeatedly. He just stands there, looking as smug as ever with his arms crossing his chest, his sharp teeth barely showing.

"Calm down. They are fine. Actually, their waiting outside. I wanted to come in first to make sure everything was . . ." he leaves unfinished, grinning evilly.

"Drake Malberry, don't you dare think of such things! I would never hurt them nor feed from them. They are my friends, not food. Why are you looking at me as if I'm an idiot? Send them in right away," I command, placing my hands stubbornly on my hips, hopefully showing dominance and power.

His head tilts questioningly at me, almost in admire, before leaving the room and returning two seconds later. "Done." He flops down on my bed without asking and just as I'm about to smack him upside the head, a shrill, musical taunting voice stops me in my tracks.

"CHLOE! My God, your awake!!" Autumn squeals, a few notches too loud. I fight back a sharp hiss, biting down on my lips to keep it from coming out. No one notices this. No one but Drake; he nods approvingly, glad I am no longer hissing and snapping at everything.

"Shh, Autty, speak lower. Lakota's ears are very sensitive now. It will take some getting used to for her," Drake speaks smoothly, sounding every bit concerned and sweet.

She covers her mouth with her hand as if to silently say oops. She's even more prettier and childlike, I thought to myself in a daze. She is like a faerie. Dylan his self is more manly appealing, more defined in my eyes. Only thing that is really different is I can smell a wild, tangy, untamed smell coming from his skin. I wouldn't call it repulsive but it did make me more curious. He catches me staring and blushes a rosy pink.

"It's the werewolf of me, I'm sorry. Would you like me to leave?" he asks in a unemotional tone, but I can hear the underlines of it. He is hurt by my scrutinizing.

"No, no. It's fine, really. Please stay. Forgive me, for I'm not used to this new sight and smell. I mean, you smell alright. It's just--that you smell different, not bad, just different," I smile at him. From the corner of my eye, I see Autumn flash me a sad, painful look that she assumes goes unnoticed by me.

"Well, you look . . .very healthy," October finally manages to pick a word, her voice dripping with envy as her eyes narrow very slightly at me, taking me in carefully.

"That's all you can say? Well, damn, she looks better than merely healthy; she's perfect. Being a Goddess and Vampyre suits you extremely well," Drake tells me, his smile free of any evil or anything dark. "Your one of the best looking woman I've ever saw."

"I agree!" Autumn chirps, grinning from ear to ear. "Don't forget--Witchans are usually beautiful too. Its like, you were designed to be-"

"Yeah, yeah, we get it--perfect," October snaps, stepping forward to give her a hateful glare. "Shouldn't you be asking more important questions like, did we win, who did we lose, how many did we lost? Not something unimportant as looks!" she bellows, blood rushing to her face. I have never seen her so, so angry and green monster filled.

"My, my, my, someone is very jealous. Ha! The much-average-and-plain-looking-October actually envies Chloe," Drake laughs, his silver eyes taunting and dark.

"She's right. How many did we lose?" I ask, somber, preparing myself for shock. They all turn to me, grinning like children on Christmas day right before they open their gifts.

"Not many," Dylan finally offers, leaning back onto the wall.

"Very few, actually. Odin came swooping in with thousands of people, ready to serve you," Autumn smiles sweetly, tilting her head in awe.

"It was a miracle. I thought for sure we'd all die, especially after seeing you collapse to the ground. At that same moment, he pops up from nowhere and so does mass other creatures of this world," October puts in, her eyes distant, looking back. It already feels like this has happened centuries ago and not days. Funny how time can fly by you so quickly . . .

"I was watching nearby, two seconds from joining when I saw him, that monster, come after you. And I knew then, you would die. I screamed out for you to watch out, but you soon enough had you eye on him. I came forth, willing to fight with you but Odin stopped me and said something odd like 'this is her and her battle alone to fight.' But oohh, when you are stabbed and fall, it's another story. He comes rushing up to you-and boy have I never seen someone move so fast like either of you!-and takes you into his arms.

"You mutter like crazy, nothing making much sense. Stuff like angel, I love you, beautiful, peaceful, I never want to leave, I'm ready to go, let me go, stuff like that. It was terrible. I had to coax him into saving your life, you know. I could see he wanted to but he wouldn't, at first. Not until you looked up at him and told him to let you go and that this was what should be. He was quick to bite you then and suddenly whoosh! You two disappear and I'm sitting alone in the middle of a freaking battle field," Drake claims, sounding under control and unmoved. The look of despair in his eyes say otherwise.

I take all this in slowly, feeling my knees go weak a second before Drake's arms are about me, holding my weight up with concern. "We need to get her to bed. Her body is still weak from the transit," I hear him mumble from far away.

"No," I cry, willing my voice to be strong and not to be ignored, but instead comes out weak and pathetic to even my own ears.

"Lakota, you need your strength. Get some rest, okay? We'll be here when you wake. Sleep," he mummers, kissing my temple and lays me on the bed, pulling the covers over me. "Sleep."

And eventually, I did sleep. It wasn't peaceful, yet it was. It was the most soul awakening, awful, beautiful, sad dream I had ever dreamt up.

"Who are you?" I ask, curiously staring up at the stranger. I wasn't really concerned though. Everything here, everything around me feel so peaceful and relaxed. Later, I wouldn't be able to remember the scenery or his face as he laughed and laughed.

"You do not recognize me? I figured everyone in your world did," he smiles simply, his eyes fixed on my face. "Your as beautiful as they say you are. And I can see strength and bravery radiating from your soul. You have a good soul-not pure, nor evil-just a decent soul. You really don't know who I am?" he stops his babbling and glances at me once again. His eyes--they show so much age, like Odin's.

With that, the dream shattered and I was in my bedroom, panting and breathing so hard I thought I was having a heart attack! "NO!" I screamed, my lungs burning.

"My God, what is wrong, Lakota?" someone asks making me jump and hiss, pulling my lips back over my teeth. "Shhh, it's only me. Odin. I felt your despair and came at once. I-I couldn't see your dreams, which is odd enough, so I waited to you come around. You must tell me what happened. Don't leave a thing out," he adds, sounding desperate and a bit crazy. His eyes were bloodshot and his hair was messed up, as if he had been tossing and turning all night.

Tears pour down my cheeks easily and I don't even know why. I leave them there and look at him eagerly. "I can't remember where I was or when. I don't think it was a vision. There was a man there with me and he kept looking and smiling at me. I can't even remember what he looked like!" I cry, taking a deep breath in and out, in and out. Within seconds I regain control over myself though my soul feels shaken and on the verge of breaking into pieces that could never be fix.

"Well, what is that?" he points to the ceiling, sounding a bit shaken up now. I throw him a confused look before I follow his finger and gasp. JULIAN SAINT DE PAUL was written in my silver blood, in a eerie yet exotic handwriting too fine and old to be mine. His, something whispered to me, cold blood runs down my back leaving goose bumps all over me. Julian Saint de Paul. So, that's who you are? A very strange name.

"I guess I wrote it," I lied, my eyes still glued to it. "Who is Julian Saint de Paul, Odin? I'm sure you would know him. I don't think he is from this world but I do not believe him to be Human. What could that mean?"

"I don't know who that is, Lakota. Your guess is as good as mine. Of course, don't be so shocked and scared. There are nine worlds in all, so he could very well belong to any of them. Was-was he shaped like a man would be?" his words are sharp and harsh, almost cruel, heartless. I shrink back into my bed.

"I think so. I really don't know. It was more like a vision of his soul more than anything," I add after a deep thought. "I'm so tired. School begins today again for me, doesn't it?" He flashes me a concerned look before masking it. "I think you need a couple of more days to rest, Lakota. Your body needs to heal from the transfusion and the war. Speaking of which, I brought you a couple of gallons. It should make you feel better instantly and last awhile, yes?" He lays one next to me on the night stand and opening it to pour it into a fancy looking glass. It fills with the pretty red liquid as the smell hits me at once before he hands it to me. "Drink. You'll feel so much better."

I eye it for a second, resisting the call of it. "Yours?"

"No. A Human's," he says emotionlessly, still holding it out.

"Why? You know I need yours for a couple of months. Your blood alone is the best for me," I shrill, rising in bed. "You drink it! I don't want it." I wanted so badly to taste his. Something deep down told me his would be the best even if we wasn't tied now. Blood is like wine--the older, the better it tastes, my gut whispers to me.

"Lakota, please, don't," he begs, sounding scared, for once meeting my eyes directly to empathize his plea. He places the glass back onto the night stand then takes my hands gently and a fire erupts from his very touch, washing over my entire body.

"Without it, I will die," I said, bringing his hands to my lips for a light, quick kiss. I feel him shudder in disgust. He snatches his hands away, standing on his feet away from me. "You MAY die without it-"

"So, you're willing to take the chance?" I accuse, more hurt than ever. I suddenly didn't want his presence, his beautiful face and body, even if it was always draped in loose clothing, I knew his beauty was all around when it concerned Odin Omay.

"No! I just don't want---I . . .You're suppose to be dead already!" he yells in anger, pacing around my chambers, his hands fingering the other. I've never seen him so bothered.

"Because of what is in my blood," I spat, growing more and more irate.

"No, no. In the war, I had clear orders centuries ago and yet, I defied them. How the High Concile will be so disappointed," he says dryly then stops, his eyes widening as he listens to my mind and what he just said.

"What do you mean, orders? Odin!" I snap when he doesn't answer right away. He flinches.

"I was given orders by the High Concile to allow the 'mixed blood' to die in the war for Humans. I will be punished very soon."

"But you didn't. You saved me . . ."

"Yes," he sighs, sitting back onto my bed. "I saved you. The end."

"Only when Drake pleaded you to," I say bitterly. "I still need your blood," I add, my voice dripping with stubbornness.

He nods, taking the glass and finishing it all down in two gulps. He then pulls his sleeve up and cuts it open with his nail quickly and swiftly as if he had done this many, many times before, pouring his jet blue blood into the glass then sets it on the night stand beside me. Appalled, my mouth hangs open. "What? Don't you know it's very un-lady like and unbecoming to leave your mouth hanging wide open," he says in a dry matter of fact tone.

"Thank you," I whisper.

He gathers to his feet as if it is difficult to do so, appearing to be every year of his age. "I must go. Get some sleep. You won't be returning to your studies until I have decided what to do about your schooling."

The only thing I could muster up is very smart, "huh?"

"Your fully Turned, Chloe. By law, you shouldn't still be here. Although, you haven't enough studies to go out into this world. There's so much more you need to know, dear, and quick. I have no doubt the High Concile will be pouncing on you soon. Now, sleep. I'll be back later to give you more of my blood." He bows respectfully before turning to the door.

"Goodnight, my Lord," I call out the most respectful and correct term to him. Since he has changed me, he has legally become my Lord. It felt so queer (and not in homosexual terms) to call him his rightful title.

Once he is out of sight, I pick up the glass filled with his hypnotizing blood and raise it to my nose, moaning at the sheer smell. Carefully, I lower it to my lips, sipping at first then hungrily gulping it down once the rush and drunken-like feeling kicks in, devowing the taste. And my God does it taste better than anything in either worlds! If he was to sell his blood, it would easily put Coke, Mountain Dew, and even those fancy dancy waters they just recently started selling, out of business the first day it goes out in the market. My eyes, my veins, my very skin, everything felt on fire, like electricity had just coursed through me and consumed me whole and I love it. I don't want this feeling, this extreme high to ever end.

I need him, something shakes inside of me. I wanted more than ever to kiss, to hold him, to touch the pearly white marble skin, to merge into one, to simply take a long gander at his beauty that's almost to much to bear. In a instant, I'm on my feet and looking for him in the long, wide corridors, knowing he must be hearing my thoughts. I turn on my feet, not really looking where I'm going until I'm standing outside of the triple doors where he trains me, taking a deep breath before I open the doors and find him standing on the far other side.

"Odin . . ." I call out in a desperate voice, causing him to turn to me.

Chapter Ten: Going Back To Basics

"Odin," I breathed again, taking a step towards the cloaked figure several hundred feet away.

"Lakota Chloe VanHoren?" the voice comes from the man and in a flash is right before me. Crap, it isn't Odin, disappointment washes through me. It's just some stranger.

"Yes?" I snap, irritated at the face it wasn't the man I wanted. The desire sinks back into my blood, leaving behind anger. He grimaces at me from what I can see in the dark.

"Your . . . Aunt," he finally settles on a word to call her, glancing at me. It doesn't surprise me that everyone has told this man the truth-that the woman who was suppose to be my aunt is actually my great-grand niece. "Her health is steadily declining. She begged me to leave you alone but we all agreed that you must return home immediately. I'm afraid she won't be alive much longer," he adds in a detached tone, looking away uncomfortably at my stare.

Aunt Sarah is dying? I thought, appalled. Yeah, right. She wouldn't allow a single bacteria or disease to enter her body and take over it. She would just easily demand it to go away. Gathering my thoughts, I say, "what is she-dying from?" It is hard to think of her as a dying patient and anything other than my aunt. That was what she was to me for the past 17 years and she will always have that title.

"Some form of cancer," he replies easily, once again emotionless. Finally, this gets to me. "Look, you may not know her but you could at least show some kind of respect towards a being! And as for cancer, that's impossible. No Immortal can get cancer. You must have it wrong. And Sarah wouldn't allow any disease to kill her off. She's far too stubborn," I almost yell at the stranger.

He smiles then hides it, as if he is afraid to show any emotions. A-ha, he does know her, I think to myself.

"The cancer she has, Immortals can get. Now, we must be on our way at once. I was ordered to watch over you during your stay in the Human realm. The High Concile told me you didn't know how to transport yet so you will have to hold onto my hand," he offers his out to me. I take it, sighing in defeat and as soon as I blink we're back in the other realm. Instantly, I let go off his hand and make my way towards the old house.

"Chloe," John exclaims, opening the door as soon as we get to it. I smile brightly at the ancient butler we've had for ages now. He looks the same as always. Surprising me, he gives me a tight, warming hug before closing the grand doors behind me. "Everyone is already here. I was waitin' and waitin' 'fore you to show up. Now that your 'ere, I can go to bed. Sarah said you was coming tonight. I got your room made up," he adds when I don't say anything. He turns to . . .what is the man's name next to me? I didn't even ask for it and he didn't offer his name. Rudeness, obnoxious guy, I grouch in my head. "Sorry, but all the other rooms are taken. You'll have to share with Chloe." At that, he walks away, winking at me. Huh. What was that about? I dismiss the thought and make my way up the curvy stairs and to my bedroom.

"Very nice," he says, taking the room in. I turn to look at him finally in the light and is shocked by what I find. A man that appears to be no older than 26, with casual clothes-blue, slightly baggy jeans and a sort-of tight white shirt. His hair is jet black and just the right length to make his looks even more enchanting. The eyes are a deep, dark intense blue that reminded you of lightning when you felt his glare on you. His skin was a naturally tanned color, his shirt displayed the easy muscles he has. He's gorgeous, I thought, feeling my body go weak. Great, yet another perfect man to make me lose my mind. Angry, I ignore him and go to my drawer to get the night clothes I had left behind. I grab the only shirt-a tank-and the only pjs I had left here-some white, cotton shorts. It'll do until I have some one send for less revealing clothes.

Once I got to the bathroom, I found a huge surprise with turning the door and stepping in. A short man with bright, striking blonde hair howled and said "welcome to Narnia! The place you never get old," he grins and I yelp, shutting the door and quickly going back to my room. The man there looks me over in a second.

"Why aren't you already changed?" he snaps, taking off his shirt and making my heart gain speed like a heroin addict. Good God, he's sexy, I bite my lip. "Lakota?" he repeats, his lips slashed in a amused smile.

"Huh? Oh, yeah. A weirdo is in there, saying that the bathroom is now Narnia and is an enchanted, wonderful land. I'll have to change here," I add, giving him a look. After a few seconds, he catches on it. I can literally see a fictional light bulb clicking on in head.

"Oh, right. Uhm, well, I'll go see to it," he awkwardly says, leaving the room. Once he is gone, I take in my room. Everything is the exact same as I had left it. The math book is still left open with a pen laying in the fold on the desk, the slippers still by the door. It looks like whoever dusted the room picked up whatever they decided to clean and put it back once it was. I could easily close my eyes and pretend I still lived here and was a na\u00efve, Human on her way to school and the only thing she had to worry about was the cute, popular boy in gym asking for a date. I sigh, pulling over the tank and pulling up the shorts. The second I'm finished, the man comes back into the room, his face flushed with anger and somewhat fear. I giggle, remembering the crash and noises I heard coming through the walls.

"How was it?" I sniffle a laugh. He glares at me, his eyes shrinking.

"As if you don't already know. The man came at me and tried to eat my ear! Saying he was Prince Captain and he wanted to have my ear wax." At that, I lost it and nearly collapsed to the ground roaring with laughter so hard, I had tears in my eyes. "Laugh all you want," he snaps and sits on the small couch. "Stay away from the bathroom from now on. What in the world are you wearing?" he hisses, his blue, blue eyes going to my small tank and shorts.

Okay, I admit, since the change I had grown in certain areas. The tank made my girlies pop out dramatically, the shorts were pulled up in the back so it showed the beginning of an area I'd much rather keep hidden from this man. I blush, crossing my arms, imaging what I probably looked right now to me. Drake would cheer and call it unbelievably sexy and seductive and judging his reactions, I would say he would agree with Drake.

"It's the only clothing I have. You made us leave without me packing anything to take with me," I point out and go to my bed, quickly getting into it. He sighs again and lays back on the uncomfortable couch. "Uhm, sir? You don't have to sleep there. There is

plenty of room here on the bed for you," I blush again and mentally smack myself.
He meets my eyes, making my heart pound again. "What would that look like to the others, Lakota? Me sleeping in the bed of a respected, high Goddess?"
"Exactly what it looks like. Us just going to sleep and nothing else," I say firmly, but knew he was right. Fine, if he wants to sleep on a small, stiff couch then I'll let him. I yawn, covering my mouth. "Ni-night."
"Good morrow," he whispers back and I close my eyes, my last thought was on Odin and where he was.
Hearing the birds chirping outside my window woke me almost instantly. I groan, turning over to feel something hard yet soft below me. I moan, my hands having a mind of their own and roaming the warm, velvety smoothness of his skin. Skin? Naked? My eyes shot open. Sure enough, the gorgeous stranger is passed out below me. Or so I thought.
"Are you going to continue laying there or are you going to get up so I can finally go to the bathroom?"
My face flushes and I remove my hands-and body-from him, feeling his arms release me.
"Seems like I wasn't the only one rolling around. I thought you went to bed on the couch," I mutter in confusion. He turns on the bed to meet my eyes directly.
"I did. I couldn't sleep for hours and remembered your offer," he says easily, his eyes blazing and smiling.
"What about not wanting to ruin my good name?"
He grins at that and shrugs, gathering to his feet and stretches before answering me. "You never really had a good reputation when it comes to men, so I figured whats one more to the long list of conquered men?"
I throw my heavier pillow at him, which he smoothly dashes it just in time without even looking at it. "That's not true! I've never woken up to a stranger in my bed before."
He laughs, seeming in a better mood now than last night. "Don't go around saying that or else people will wonder what you smoked or drinked last night."
I grin back at him, folding my arms across my chest. "You don't have to worry about that. I wouldn't want anyone to think Lakota VanHoren has lowered her standards in men," I retort. He howls in laughter, his eyes twinkling again.
"So you think. I've never been conceited but I can at least say I'm better looking than Dylan Blackwood and Drake Malbury, although Lucifer is, undeniably better."
My heart stops, the blood leaves my face. "Drake, Dylan?" I whisper in shock. What was everyone saying about me behind my back?
"Well, yeah. There are rumors your sleeping with the devil, the devil's son, and a werewolf. A nice range of different men, I'd say, but you do seem to like the unavailable ones, don't you?" he nearly hisses, looking angry. Oh, great, another racist man.
"I'm not sleeping with Drake nor Dylan! It's against the law to with Dylan and I don't even talk to Drake anymore. We never even went close to doing it," I snap, getting in his face. Relief washes over his face before it is clouded again.
"I believe you but you didn't deny the charges with Lucifer, did you?" he mutters bitterly, snatching my wrist when I went to turn away. "I have to know."
"Why? Why would it matter to you? I don't even know your name yet your demanding to know my sex life! Yet, I don't care-it is in the past. Yes, me and Luce had sex a few

times, twice is all. I haven't seen him lately and I don't care to either."

He nods and lets go off the tight hold on me. I rub at it, giving him glares.

"I'm your body guard while we are in this realm. I have to know the people that will come calling on you. My name is Lu-naren Comprez," he offers his hand to shake with mine. I do so out of respect.

"Why do I need protection here and not in the other world?"

"Odin protects you there and since he cannot make this trip, I have been hired to watch over you in the mean time. People want you dead, Lakota," he says, like a booming.

"Yeah, that's not a shocker," I sigh, running my fingers through my hair, sighing again because it felt greasy and tangled. "All my clothes are in Otherworld. I can't go see Aunt Sarah like this," I mumble. Lu stares at me for a few seconds then makes patterns in the air and whispers in a beautiful, foreign language, almost the exact dialect I've heard Odin speak in. In his hands appears simple clothing-a white shirt, and a very modest blue skirt with a hair brush laying on top of the neatly folded clothes.

"Holy crap, how did you do that!" I nearly shout at him, making him grin even wider and shrug his shoulders. I take the clothes eagerly; it's better than nothing. "And a skirt, really?"

"Oh hush, you'd look out of place in this world if you were to wear pants like a man and it's called magick for a reason. No, I'm not a warlock," he adds when I go to ask him.

He has a point about the skirt but still, I hate them. I don't care if I get shunned for wearing pants here. "Then what are you?"

"Your body guard," he replies easily, looking away. Huh. "C'mon, get dressed already. I'll meet you in Sarah's room, okay?" he shuts the door behind him. In minutes I am trailing after him, still fidgeting about the skirt and mumbling disagreements about it. Why is he so secretive? Better yet, why did he get so nervous when I asked what he was? Not that it really matters to me, but I think he is a God or something that is truly Immortal.

"Come in," says a raspy, drained voice when I knock on Aunt Sarah's doors. "My, you have grown, child! Even your eyes-they speak more of maturity and wisdom. I am proud to hear that you are doing so well in Otherworld," she whispers, smiling weakly. My eyes instantly water up as I take in her appearance.

While I have grown, she has shrunk considerably. Though she was always short, she somehow appeared shorter, and lost a lot of weight. She was wearing a low cut shirt and I could see bones sticking out from every direction. She weighs no more than 80 pounds now! Even her hair had more silver streaks and lost it's thickness. She was losing majority of her hair. Her eyes appeared much larger and flat-void of any emotions. I stumbled up to her beside, lost for words.

"Shh, do not frit, girl. I'll be okay. The worst is already over. I'm not in much pain anymore. It has been going on for awhile and I wanted to tell you, I really did, but I couldn't-you had too much going on in your own life as is. You didn't need anymore distractions," she stops, her chest pulling in and out as she gasped for breath. A tear spills over finally but I don't bother to wipe it away. A shaky hand reaches out to wipe it but fails miserably.

"You could have told me at least! Your more important than some stupid war!" I cried, turning away from her so she couldn't see my sorrow. I was more hurt that I was losing her than I was mad at her. I couldn't help yelling at her.

"No. No, I'm not and you know it Lakota Chloe VanHoren. What's one person compared to all of mankind? Jul, did you not come in here alone?" she addressed Lu, her snappy tone, her old self, coming back for just a second.

"Yes, I did," he looks down, humbled by her. She hisses at him, baring her teeth, leaning up weakly.

"If I were healthier, I'd smack you. Some body guard you are! You were ordered to stay by her side no matter what, correct? No, don't answer that. I don't want to hear pathetic responses and empty apologizes. Give me both of your hands," she adds after a few moments of silence. We both give her what she wants, only his eyes widen at her.

"What are you-"

"Shush, boy!" she yells, then begins in that same ancient language I've heard her mumble in for years. Our hands lite up a bright red in the middle of our palms and suddenly, just as quickly as the light came, it was gone and replaced it was warmth. She lays back, breathing heavily with sweat dripping down her face and chest. "Leave me be, I'll speak to you later," she nods at me, then a slow smile forms on her thin, pale lips, looking eerie.

"Oh, Mama, please, can I go outside to play with Thomas and all the others? I promise I won't mess up my clothing, I promise!" she says in a child-like voice, her eyes glazed over and fixed at something that wasn't there.

"Aunt Sarah? You okay? Aunt Sarah," I repeat, stepping closer to her but Lu stops me, his eyes showing clear sadness.

"She's a bit out of it. Let us leave her in peace for now. Hopefully, she'll be better later," he takes on last look at her before shutting the door.

"Right. I'm hungry, I'm going to go-" I gasp, reaching to my neck, trying to get air. I-just-couldn't-breath! My body, my veins, everything is on fire. Dear God, this is what it means to truly burn in Hell, I just know it! But, I could breath again and the burning, it went away! Lu was breathing quickly right by me.

"FUCK!" he yelled, his face red and furious. "That cunning, old witch! I knew I shouldn't have trusted her for one single second, not one. Ohh, the irony!" he clenches his chest, his face distorted in pain.

"What, what is it? And what in the world was that?" I ask, afraid now. What had Aunt Sarah done to us?

"That woman," he spats hatefully, "she put a binding spell on us. We can't be more than ten feet from each other. She did it so I could be linked to you and keep a better watch over you, as retribution for not being up your buttocks every minute."

I frown, not liking this idea at all. I needed to take a shower, did she think about that? Oh. My. Goodness. We are screwed. The blood leaves my face as realization hits me. Aunt Sarah won't be able to even undo the spell for a long time and even then, she could pass at any moment now. "We need to get this off of us immediately."

He looks at me oddly then goes to speak when a bright, flashing white light pops up next to me. Once the light is gone, I can see three men-or people-standing before me with black cloaks on and their face is hidden by their hoods.

"Lakota VanHoren?" one asks, his voice flat and void. I frown in confusion. They shouldn't be able to trespass on private grounds.

"Yes, this is her. What do you want?"

They step up to me, grabbing my hands swifty, causing Lu to growl. "You are being arrested for three counts of treason of Otherworld and allegedly seducing a man of the Church. Back away from her, Julian," one says to him in a hiss.

"Julian? No, that is Lu, you have the wrong guy. Wha-how am I being arrested! I didn't sleep with a man of any devoted religion. Please, you have to believe me!" I shrill, but they ignore me anyways and hand cuff me with golden cuffs.

"You will have a fair trial and you have the right to have a counsel present when questioning. Anything you say can be used against you in the court and for evidence."

"Wait, she needs her things from Otherworld!" Lu or Julian says. Who is he really? Something asked in the pits of my stomach but I push the thought out of my head and focus on remaining silent. "We have a binding. Wherever she goes, I have to go or we'll both die."

"Very well, Julian. We shall allow you to go, for now. Remove the hand cuffs," the tallest one orders to the others. They step up quickly, removing the golden things. I sigh of relief, for the gold had been burning my hands.

Lu makes my things pop out of nowhere and grins at me, winking then looks to the ground somber again. Everything is already packed and ready to go. The tall one grabs my arm roughly and begins to drag me outside. A limo is waiting for us. A limo, really, for a criminal? That's strange as Hell. Odin is waiting for us by the car, his face alerted, not even bothering to look at me.

"I am sorry this has to happen, Lakota," he grumbles, almost blushing.

"Well, yeah, me too, Odin, me too. I don't even know what I have done that was so wrong!" I cry, a tear finally letting loose.

"Just--say you're sorry publicly and everything will be forgiven. They will let you go," he begs, shooting daggers at the three men. "Just apologize to our country."

"I have done nothing wrong, I will not say sorry," I snap, feeling strong and powerful as they pull me back away from him and into the car. This isn't so bad, it really isn't, I try convincing myself. At least Lu will be with you and you'll have someone to talk to, to see. What's going to happen to me? I thought as the car pulled away and a single tear streaks down my cheek. I don't bother to wipe it away, too lost in my thoughts to even care about it. May God have mercy on me. . . .

The end, for now (:

yes
i want morebooks!

Buy your books fast and straightforward online - at one of world's fastest growing online book stores! Environmentally sound due to Print-on-Demand technologies.

Buy your books online at

www.get-morebooks.com

Kaufen Sie Ihre Bücher schnell und unkompliziert online – auf einer der am schnellsten wachsenden Buchhandelsplattformen weltweit! Dank Print-On-Demand umwelt- und ressourcenschonend produziert.

Bücher schneller online kaufen

www.morebooks.de

VDM Verlagsservicegesellschaft mbH
Heinrich-Böcking-Str. 6-8   Telefon: +49 681 3720 174   info@vdm-vsg.de
D - 66121 Saarbrücken   Telefax: +49 681 3720 1749   www.vdm-vsg.de

Printed by Books on Demand GmbH, Norderstedt / Germany